"Tender and gentle, with two delightful characters who truly belong together. A lovely read."
—RaeAnne Thayne

* * *

"Are you saying you'll help me?"

"Are you going to keep throwing things at me?" he asked.

"That was an accident."

"Accidents seem to happen around you often."

"I thought you were going to apologize."

"Fannie, please accept my apology for calling you crazy."

"All right. I forgive you."

"*Danki.* Now it's your turn."

"For what?"

"For calling me a *dummkopf.*"

"Lots of Amish folks have nicknames. That's mine for you."

He threw his hands in the air. "What am I even doing here?"

She caught hold of his arm. "I'm sorry. Will you help me?"

"I think a pretend courtship could be in my best interest as well as yours."

She squealed, "Noah, I could hug you right now."

He held out both hands. "Drop the pitchfork first."

After thirty-five years as a nurse, **Patricia Davids** hung up her stethoscope to become a full-time writer. She enjoys spending her free time visiting her grandchildren, doing some long-overdue yard work and traveling to research her story locations. She resides in Wichita, Kansas. Pat always enjoys hearing from her readers. You can visit her online at patriciadavids.com.

Books by Patricia Davids

Love Inspired

The Amish Bachelors

An Amish Harvest
An Amish Noel
His Amish Teacher
Their Pretend Amish Courtship

Lancaster Courtships

The Amish Midwife

Brides of Amish Country

The Christmas Quilt
A Home for Hannah
A Hope Springs Christmas
Plain Admirer
Amish Christmas Joy
The Shepherd's Bride
The Amish Nanny
An Amish Family Christmas: A Plain Holiday
An Amish Christmas Journey
Amish Redemption

Visit the Author Profile page at Harlequin.com for more titles.

Their Pretend Amish Courtship

Patricia Davids

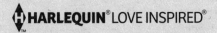
HARLEQUIN® LOVE INSPIRED®

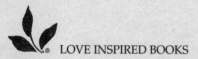

LOVE INSPIRED BOOKS

Recycling programs for this product may not exist in your area.

ISBN-13: 978-0-373-89932-6

Their Pretend Amish Courtship

Copyright © 2017 by Patricia MacDonald

www.Harlequin.com

Printed in U.S.A.

And God hath set some in the church,
first apostles, secondarily prophets,
thirdly teachers, after that miracles,
then gifts of healings, helps, governments,
diversities of tongues.
—*1 Corinthians* 12:28

This book is lovingly dedicated to my father,
Clarence Stroda. He taught me a lot
about making my way in the world
and keeping God in my life. Thanks, Dad.

Chapter One

"You are going and I don't want to hear another word about it, Fannie. Nor from you, Betsy. Do you hear me?"

When Fannie's mother shook a wooden spoon at one or both of her daughters, the conversation was over.

"*Ja, Mamm.*" Betsy beat a quick retreat out of the kitchen.

Fannie glared after her. The little coward. Without her sister's help, Fannie had no chance of changing her mother's mind. Seated at the table in her family's kitchen, Fannie crossed her arms on the red-checkered tablecloth and laid her head on her forearms. "*Ja, Mamm,* I hear you."

There had to be a way. There just had to be.

"Now you are being sensible." Belinda Erb turned back to the stove and continued stirring the strawberry jam she was getting ready to can.

"I will write to my *mamm* and *daed* tomorrow. They insist on sending the money for your bus ticket. I expect you'll be able to leave the middle of next week. It will be a relief to know one of us is helping *Daed* look after *Mamm* while she recovers from her broken ankle."

"A week! That isn't much time to get ready to go to Florida." How was she going to come up with a plan to keep from going in a week?

"Nonsense. It's plenty of time. You have two work dresses and a good Sunday dress. What else do you need?"

Fannie sat up and touched her head covering. "I need another *kapp* or two."

Her mother turned around with a scowl on her face. "What happened to the last one I made you?"

"I lost it."

"When you were out riding like some wild child, no doubt. It's time you gave up your childish ways. Anna Bowman and I were just talking about this yesterday. We have been too lenient with our youngest *kinder*, and we are living to rue the day. She is putting her foot down with Noah, and I am doing the same with you. When you come back from Pinecraft at Thanksgiving, you will end your *rumspringa* and make your decision to be Amish or not."

Fannie had heard about Anna's plans to see

Noah settled and she felt sorry for him, but she had her own problems.

Her mother turned back to the stove. "I have given up on seeing you wed, though it breaks my heart to say so."

Here came the lecture about becoming an old maid. She wasn't twenty-two yet, but she had been hearing this message since she turned nineteen. That was how old her mother had been when she married. Why did everyone believe the only thing a woman wanted was a husband? "Betsy isn't married and she is two years older than I am."

"Betsy is betrothed to Hiram. They will marry next fall."

Fannie sat up straight. "When did this happen?"

Why hadn't her sister mentioned it? Betsy and Hiram had been walking out together for ages. Fannie thought Hiram would never get up the courage to propose.

"Hiram came to tell your father and me last night."

"Then why does Betsy want to go to Florida?"

Fannie's mother took her time before answering. "She loves her grandparents and wishes to spend time with them while she can. As you should."

After pulling the jam off the stove, Fannie's

mother came and sat beside her at the table. "Why are you so dead set against going?"

Fannie knew her mother wouldn't approve of the promise she'd made. "I have made plans with my riding club for this summer."

"Your horses and your club won't take care of you when you are old. *Mamm* writes that there are plenty of young people in Pinecraft during the fall and winter. You may want to stay longer."

"Young people but no horses."

"Enough about horses!" Fannie's mother rose to her feet. "You have chores to finish and I must get these jars of jam done. It's a wedding gift for Timothy Bowman and his bride. Timothy's mother told me they plan to leave on their wedding trip after the school frolic."

Fannie clamped her lips together. Her mother wanted to change the subject. It wouldn't do any good to argue; Fannie knew she'd only be wasting her breath. She left the room and found her sister gathering clothes off the line in the backyard. Fannie joined her, pulling down stiff winddried pants and dresses. "*Mamm* said you went and got engaged to Hiram."

"It was time. I'm not getting any younger."

"That's a poor reason to marry."

"It's reason enough for us. We are content with each other. You are blessed to have this opportunity." Betsy clutched a pillowcase to her chest.

"I have always dreamed of seeing the ocean. I can't imagine how big it must be. Hiram has no desire to see the sea."

"Doesn't he have a desire to please you?" That, in a nutshell, was what was wrong with getting married.

"It would be an expense we couldn't afford. Perhaps someday."

"I would gladly send you in my place, but I don't imagine Hiram would be happy about...that..." Fannie's words trailed away as an idea took shape in her mind. "That's it. I need a Hiram."

"What are you babbling about now?"

It was so simple. "Betsy, would you go to Florida if I couldn't? What if *Mamm* decided you should go instead of me? Would Hiram understand?"

"He knows we must honor our elders. I would gladly take your place, but *Mamm* has her mind made up."

"If she knew I was being courted, she would bend over backward to keep me here. She is desperate to see me wed."

"She's desperate to see you interested in any young man instead of your horses. Who is courting you? Why didn't you tell me about him?"

"I have to go." Fannie shoved the clothes in her arms at her sister. There was only one fellow who might help her.

* * *

"Noah, where are you? I need to speak to you."

Working near the back of his father's barn, Noah Bowman dropped the hoof of his buggy horse, Willy, took the last nail out of his mouth and stood upright to stare over his horse's back. Fannie Erb, his neighbor's youngest daughter, came hurrying down the wide center aisle, checking each stall as she passed. Her white *kapp* hung off the back of her head, dangling by a single bobby pin. Her curly red hair was still in a bun, but it was windblown and lopsided. No doubt it would be completely undone before she got home. Fannie was always in a rush.

"What's up, *karotte oben*?" He picked up his horse's hoof again, positioned it between his knees and drove in the last nail of the new shoe.

Fannie stopped outside the stall gate and fisted her hands on her hips. "You know I hate being called a carrottop."

"Sorry." Noah grinned as he caught the glare she leveled at him.

He wasn't sorry a bit. He liked the way her unusual violet eyes darkened and flashed when she was annoyed. Annoying Fannie had been one of his favorite pastimes when they were schoolchildren.

She lived on the farm across the road where her family raised and trained Standardbred buggy horses. Noah had known her from the cradle, as their parents were good friends and often visited back and forth. Fannie had grown from the gangly girl he liked to tease at school into a comely woman, but her temper hadn't cooled.

Framed in a rectangle of light cast by the early-morning sun shining through the open top of a Dutch door, dust motes danced around Fannie's head like fireflies drawn to the fire in her hair. The summer sun had expanded the freckles on her upturned nose and given her skin a healthy glow, but Fannie didn't tan the way most women did. Her skin always looked cool and creamy. As usual, she was wearing blue jeans and riding boots under her plain green dress and black apron.

He preferred wearing *Englisch* jeans himself. He liked having hip pockets to keep his cell phone in, something his homemade Amish pants didn't have. His parents tolerated his use of a phone because he was still in his *rumspringa*. He knew Fannie used a cell phone, too. She had a solar-powered charger and allowed other Amish youth to use it if they didn't have access to electricity.

"What do you need, Fannie? Did your hot temper spark a fire and you want me to put it out?" He chuckled at his own wit. He and his four brothers were volunteer members of the local fire department. Patting Willy's sleek black neck, Noah reached to untie the horse's halter.

"This isn't a joke, Noah. I need to get engaged, and quickly. Will you help me?"

He spun around to stare at her in shocked disbelief. A marriage proposal was the last thing he'd expected from Fannie. "You had better explain that remark."

"*Mamm* and *Daed* are sending me to live with my grandparents in Pinecraft, Florida, until Thanksgiving. I can't go. I've told my folks that, but they insist. Having a steady beau is the only way to get them to send Betsy instead."

At least Fannie wasn't suffering from some unrequited love for him. He should have been relieved, but he was mildly annoyed instead.

He opened the bottom half of the Dutch door leading to the corral and let his horse out. Willy quickly trotted to where Fannie's Haflinger mare stood on the other side of the fence. The black gelding put his head over the top rail to sniff noses with the golden-chestnut beauty.

Noah began picking up his tools. "I hear Florida is nice."

Fannie grabbed the top of the gate. "Are you serious? My grandparents get around on three-wheeled bicycles down there. They don't have horses. Can you imagine staying in a place with no horses?"

He couldn't, but he didn't think much of her crazy idea, either. "I'm not going to get hitched to you because you don't want to go to Florida."

Indignation sparked in her eyes. "What's wrong with getting hitched to me? I'd make you a *goot* wife."

She stepped back as he opened the stall gate. "Fannie, you would knock me on the head with a skillet the first chance you got. You have a bad temper."

"Oh!" She stomped her foot, and then sighed heavily. "I do have a temper, but I wouldn't do you physical harm."

"Small consolation considering how sharp your tongue is. Ouch! Ow!" He jumped away from several imaginary jabs.

Her eyes narrowed. "Stop teasing. I don't want to actually marry you, *dummkopf.* I said *engaged,* not *married,* but I guess it doesn't have to be that serious. Walking out with me might do. If not, we can get engaged later. Anyway, we will call it off long before the *banns* are announced and go our merry ways."

He didn't like being called a dumbhead, but he overlooked her comment to point out the biggest flaw in her plan. "You and I have never acted like a loving couple. Your parents would smell a rat."

"Maybe, but maybe not. *Mamm* has been telling me for ages that it's time I started looking around for a husband."

He closed the stall gate and latched it. "Better go farther afield for that search. The boys around here all know you too well."

She wasn't the kind of woman he'd marry. He might enjoy teasing that quick temper, but he wouldn't want to live with it.

Her defiant expression crumpled. She hurried to keep up with him as he went outside. "Don't be mean, Noah. I need help. I can't go to Florida. My *daed* has two mares due to foal this month."

"They will foal without you, and your father can certainly handle it."

She walked to her mare standing patiently beside the corral. "Trinket will miss me. I can't go months without seeing her."

Fannie loved horses, he knew that, but he sensed she wasn't telling him the whole story behind this scheme. "Trinket will survive without you. What's the real reason you don't want to go?"

She sighed heavily and folded her arms tightly across her chest. "You may have heard I took a job working for Connie Stroud on her horse farm."

"*Mamm* mentioned it." His mother kept up on all the local news. How she was able to learn so much about the community without the use of a forbidden telephone was a mystery to him.

"Connie raises and trains Haflingers. Trinket was one of her foals. Connie's father passed away two years ago and she is having a hard time making a go of the place. She gives riding lessons and boards horses, but she needs to sell more of her Haflingers for a better price than she can get around here if she is going to make ends meet."

"If she can't sell a horse without you in the state, she's a poor businesswoman."

He walked over to two more horses tied to the fence. One was his niece Hannah's black pony, Hank. The other was Ginger, a bay mare that belonged to his mother. Speaking softly to Hank, Noah ran his hand down the pony's neck and lifted his front foot. He found the shoe was loose and too worn to save. He checked the pony's back foot, expecting to find it in the same condition.

Fannie walked over to Hank and began to rub him behind his ears. The pony closed his eyes in bliss and leaned into her fingers. "I'm deeply beholden to Connie. I need to help her save her stable."

Noah glanced at Fannie's face and was surprised by the determination in her eyes. Fannie might be hotheaded and stubbornly independent, but she was clearly loyal to this friend. "How does pretending to be engaged help her?"

"It keeps me here. Not a lot of people know what amazing horses Haflingers are. I came up with the great idea of an equine drill team using Connie's Haflingers plus my Trinket. We are going to give exhibitions at some of the county fairs and then at the Ohio State Equine Expo. I have seven Amish girls from my riding club who have already joined us."

"Your parents are permitting this?" It was an unusual undertaking for an Amish woman.

She looked away from him. "We haven't been told we can't do it. You know how crazy the *Englisch* are for anything Amish. If we can generate some interest, show what Connie's horses can do, I know it will help her sell more of them. Besides, everyone in the group is depending on me to teach them—and the horses—the routines. Our first show is in a week."

Fannie had a way with horses that was unique. He'd always admired that about her. "I'm sure your parents will come around if you make them see how much you want to stay."

"*Mamm* won't. She has her mind made up. She says Betsy is more help to her than I am because I'm always out in the barn. Betsy likes to cook, sew, mend and clean, while I don't. I'll die down there if I have to give up my horse." Fannie sniffled and wiped her eyes with the back of her hand.

Noah put Hank's hoof down to stare at Fannie. He considered putting his arm around her shoulders to comfort her, but thought better of it. "Would it help if I talked to your folks?"

"*Nee*, it won't do any good. *Mamm* will know I put you up to it."

"I'm sorry, Fannie, but don't you think your idea is a bit dishonest?"

She shook her head. "If you ask to court me today, *actually ask me*, then it won't be a lie. I can tell *Mamm* we are walking out with a straight face and a clear conscience."

"I don't see how, when you concocted the whole thing."

"You have to help me, Noah. I don't know what else to do. Betsy would *love* to spend a few months with our grandparents and see the ocean. You don't have to tell anyone you are dating me. All you have to do is take me home after the singing on Sunday and I'll do the rest. Please?"

Why did she have to sound so desperate?

Fannie wasn't making enough headway in swaying Noah. She took a deep breath and pulled out her last tool of persuasion. "What are your plans for this summer?"

He looked suspicious at her abrupt change of topic. "We are putting up hay this week. We'll start cultivating the corn after that if the rain holds off."

"I didn't mean farmwork. Are you playing ball again this summer?" She flicked the brim of the blue ball cap he wore instead of the traditional Amish straw hat. Once he chose baptism, he would have to give up his worldly dress.

He ducked away from her hand. "I'm in the league again with the fellas from the fire department. I'm their pitcher. If we keep winning like we have been, we have a shot at getting into the state invitational tournament."

She twined her fingers in Hank's mane. "You must practice a lot."

"Twice a week with games every Saturday. In fact, we have a makeup game tonight with the Berlin team, as we were rained out last weekend."

"You wouldn't mind missing a few of your practices or even a game for a family picnic or party, would you?"

"What are you getting at, Fannie?"

"I'm not the only one you'll be helping if you go out with me. Your mother has been shopping around for a wife for you. Did you know that?"

His expression hardened. "You're *narrisch*. Up until this minute I was starting to feel sorry for you."

She almost wavered, but she couldn't let Connie down. "I'm not crazy. With all your brothers married, you are the last chick in the nest."

"So?"

"So she's worried that you are still running around instead of settling down. She has asked a number of her friends to invite their nieces and granddaughters to visit this summer with the express notion of finding *you* a wife among them. They'll be here for picnics and dinners and singings all summer long, so you can size them up."

"*Mamm* wouldn't do that." Amish parents rarely meddled in their children's courtships.

"Well, she has."

"My mother isn't the meddling sort. At least, not very often."

Fannie shrugged. "Mothers are funny that way. They don't believe we can be happy unless we are married, when you and I both know we are perfectly happy being single. Are you ready to spend the summer dodging a string of desperate-to-be-wed maidens?"

"*Nee*, and that includes you and your far-fetched scheme. No one will believe I'm dating you of my own free will."

She felt the heat rush to her face. "You kissed me once."

He arched one eyebrow. "As I remember, you weren't happy about it."

"I was embarrassed that your brother Luke saw

us. I regretted my behavior afterward, and I have told you I was sorry."

"Not half as sorry as I was," he snapped back. "That glass of punch you poured on me was cold."

She *was* sorry that evening ended so badly. It had been a nice kiss. Her first.

She and Noah had slipped outside for a breath of fresh air near the end of a Christmas cookie exchange at his parent's house the winter before last. She had been curious to find out what it would be like to be kissed by him. Things had been going well in his mother's garden until Luke came by. When Noah tried for a second kiss after his brother walked away, she had been so flustered that she upended a glass of cold strawberry punch in his lap.

"That was ages ago. Are you going to berate me again or are you going to help me?" Fannie demanded.

He leaned over the pony's back, his expression dead serious. "Find some other gullible fellow."

Her temper flared and she didn't try to quell it. "Oh! You're just plain mean. See if I ever help you out of a jam. You were my last hope, Noah Bowman. If I wasn't Amish I might actually hate you for this, but I have to say I forgive you. Have fun meeting all your prospective brides this summer." She spun on her heel and mounted her horse.

"If I'm your last hope, Fannie Erb, that says more about you than it does about me," he called out as she turned Trinket around.

She nudged her mare into a gallop and blinked back tears. She didn't want him to see how deeply disappointed she was.

Now what was she going to do?

Chapter Two

❧

Noah regretted his parting comment as he watched Fannie ride away. She didn't have many friends. She was more at ease around horses than people. Her reputation as a hothead was to blame but he knew there wasn't any real harm in her. Her last bobby pin came loose as she rode off. Her *kapp* fluttered to the ground in the driveway.

Willy raised his head and neighed loudly. He clearly wanted the pretty, golden-chestnut mare with the blond mane to come back.

"Don't be taken in by good looks, Willy. A sweet disposition lasts far longer than a pretty face. I don't care what Fannie says—*Mamm* isn't in a hurry to see me wed."

He walked out and picked up Fannie's *kapp*. At the sound of a wagon approaching, he stuffed it into his back pocket. His cousins Paul and Mark Bowman drove in from the hayfield with a load of bales stacked shoulder high on a trailer pulled by Noah's father's gray Percheron draft horses. The *chug-chug* sound of the gas-powered bailer could be heard in the distance where Noah's father was pulling it with a four-horse hitch. Noah's brothers Samuel and Timothy were hooking the bales from the back of the machine and stacking them on a second trailer.

"Who was that?" Mark asked.

"Fannie Erb." Noah watched her set her horse at the stone wall bordering her family's lane. Trinket sailed over it easily.

"She rides well," Paul said with a touch of admiration in his voice.

"She does," Noah admitted.

"What did she want?" Mark asked.

Noah shook his head at the absurdness of her idea. "She's looking for a beau. Are you interested?"

Mark shook his head. "*Nee*, I'm not. I have a girlfriend back home."

His brother Paul nudged him with an elbow. "A man can go to an auction without buying a horse. It doesn't hurt to look and see what's out there."

Mark and Paul had come from Bird-In-Hand, Pennsylvania, to stay with Noah's family and apprentice with Noah's father in the family's woodworking business. The shop was closed for a few days until the Bowmans had their hay in, and Noah was glad for the extra help.

Mark scowled at his brother. "A man who doesn't need a horse but goes to the auction anyway is wasting a day *Gott* has given him. You know what they say about idle hands."

"I won't suffer from idle hands today— today—today. I'll have the blisters—blisters— blisters to prove it," Paul called out in a singsong voice. The fast-talking young man was learning to become an auctioneer.

Mark maneuvered the hay wagon next to the front of the barn. The wide hayloft door was open above them, with a bale elevator positioned in the center of it. Noah pulled the cord on the elevator's gas-powered engine. It sprang to life, and the conveyer belt began to move upward. Noah glanced toward the house and saw his brother Joshua jogging toward them. Noah sat on the belt and rode up to the hayloft. Joshua came up the same way and the two men waited for the bales their cousins unloaded.

After stacking the first thirty-five bales deep in the recesses of the hayloft, Noah and Joshua moved to the open loft door to wait for the next trailer load to come in from the field.

Joshua fanned his face with his straw hat and then mopped his sweaty brow with his handkerchief. "It's going to be another hot one."

The interior of the barn loft would be roasting by late afternoon, even with the doors open. Noah pulled off his ball cap and reached into his back pocket for his handkerchief, but pulled out Fannie's *kapp* instead.

The silly goose. Did she really think he would agree to court her at a moment's notice? Only she could come up with such a far-fetched scheme. He tucked her *kapp* back in his pocket and wiped his face with his sleeve, determined to stop thinking about her.

He leaned out of the loft to see how close the second wagon was to being full. "Looks like I'll have time to finish putting a new horseshoe on Hank before they get here. We have some pony-size shoes, don't we?"

Joshua nodded. "On the wall in the tack room. I had John Miller make a full set for Hank right after I brought him home."

"Goot."

"I can take care of him later," Joshua offered.

"Checking the horses' feet is my job. I only have Hank and Ginger left."

"What does Ginger need?"

"I noticed she was limping out in the pasture. I haven't had a chance to see why."

"I can take care of her. I know you want to have your work done before you head to your ball game."

"Danki, bruder."

"You can return the favor some other time. I'm looking forward to your game next weekend. It should be a *goot* one. Walter Osborn can knock the hide off a baseball when he connects."

Walter was an English neighbor and volunteer fire fighter. Part of his job was to gather the Amish volunteers in the area and deliver them to the fire station when the call went out. He was also a good friend of Noah's.

"Walter is the best catcher in the league and our power hitter. If we can get into the state tournament, he'll have a chance at being scouted by the pros. Those men don't come to these backwater places. Walter deserves a chance to show what he's got."

Joshua settled his hat on his head. "Are you hoping to be scouted by a pro team?"

"Where'd you get that idea?" Noah avoided looking at his brother. He'd never told anyone about his dream.

"*Mamm* and *Daed* were talking about it the other day. Your coach has been telling everyone you have a gift. It's easy to see how much you love the game, but you'll have to stop playing soon. You will be twenty-two this fall. Your *rumspringa* can't go on forever."

Noah gave the answer he always gave. "I intend

to enjoy a few more years of my running-around time before I take my vows. I'm in no rush."

Giving up his English clothes, his cell phone and the other worldly things he could enjoy now would be easy. But could he give up the game? That would be tough. He loved playing ball. Out on the pitcher's mound, with the pressure mounting, he felt alive.

He suspected that Fannie felt much the same way about her horses. She would hate giving up her riding but she would have to one day. Riding a horse astride was considered worldly and only tolerated before baptism. A rush of sympathy for her surprised him.

He pushed thoughts of Fannie and her problems to the back of his mind as he climbed down the ladder in the barn's interior and headed to the tack room. He needed to concentrate on winning the game tonight. It would bring him one step closer to his goal.

To find out if he was good enough to play professional ball.

If he was good enough, he believed it would be a sign from God to go out into the world and use his gift. If he didn't have the level of talent that his coach thought he did, that would be a sign, too. A sign that God wanted him to remain in his Amish community. Either choice would be hard but he had faith that God would show him the right path.

He was finishing Hank's shoeing when he heard the sound of a buggy coming up the lane. His mother and his sister-in-law Rebecca pulled to a stop beside him in Rebecca's buggy.

His mother graced him with a happy smile from the driver's seat. "We have just heard the nicest news."

"What would that be?" He opened the corral gate and turned Hank in with the other horses. The second hay wagon was on its way.

"The bishop's wife told me two of her nieces have arrived to spend a month visiting them. I have invited them to supper this evening," his mother said quickly.

"And I received a letter telling me my cousins from Indiana are coming to visit." Rebecca smiled at the baby in her arms. "I'll certainly be glad to have a pair of mother's helpers with me for a few months. This little fellow and his brother wear me out."

"So, both your cousins are girls?" he asked trying not to appear uneasy. Had Fannie been right?

His mother exchanged a coy glance with Rebecca. "They are, and all the young women are near your age. I'm sure you'll enjoy getting to know them. Maybe one will catch your eye. I might even talk your father into hosting a few picnics and singings this summer. Won't that be *wunderbar*?"

"Sounds like fun, but you know I'll be gone a lot this summer, and I have a ball game this evening."

His mother frowned. "It won't hurt you to miss one of your silly games. I insist you join us for supper and meet the bishop's nieces."

"The team is depending on me. I can't cancel now. It's important to them."

A stern expression settled over his mother's face. "And this is more important. Noah Bowman, we need to have a talk."

His heart sank when his mother stepped out of the buggy. She rarely took the lead in family matters. Normally his father took him aside for a talk after some indiscretion. Rebecca drove the buggy on to the house, leaving them alone.

His mother folded her arms over her chest. "Your father and I have spoken about this and prayed about it, and we have come to a decision. My *sohn*, you are our youngest. Your father and I have been lenient with you, letting you dress fancy and not plain, letting you travel with your team and keep your cell phone, but you are old enough to put away these childish things as all your brothers have done. It's time you gave serious thought to finding a wife."

He leaned close trying to cajole her with his

smile. He didn't want her to worry about a decision he couldn't make yet, so he told her what he thought she wanted to hear. "You don't have to worry about me, *Mamm*. I plan to join the church in due time. If that is *Gott*'s will."

"You give lip service to this most solemn matter, but nothing in your actions gives me cause to believe your words."

He took a step back. She was dead serious. If his parents forbade his ball playing, he would have to do as they asked or leave home. He wasn't ready to make that choice.

The odds of getting picked up by a major-league team were a thousand to one against him, but he needed to know if he was good enough. Why had God given him this talent, if not to use it?

What could he say that would change his mother's mind?

He shoved his hands into his hip pockets and rocked back on his heels. His fingers touched Fannie's *kapp*. Would she still agree to a courtship or had he burned that bridge with his taunting?

Swallowing hard, he pulled the *kapp* from his pocket and wound the ribbons around his fingers. "I didn't want to say anything, but I have plans to see someone before my game tonight."

His mother glanced from his face to the head covering in his hand. "Who?"

"Fannie. Fannie Erb."

His mother's eyes brightened as she smiled widely. She took his face between her hands and kissed his cheek. "Oh, you sweet boy. You don't know how happy I am to hear this. The daughter of my dearest friend. Why didn't you tell me?"

"I thought I had a plan to stay, but it fell through." Fannie and Connie had finished exercising two of Connie's horses and were brushing them down before returning them to their stalls.

"What plan was that?"

"I asked Noah Bowman to pretend to court me and he turned me down." Fannie patted Goldenrod's sleek neck and ran her fingers through the mare's cream-colored mane. She hated to admit her failure to her friend.

Connie swept a lock of shoulder-length blond hair away from her face and gave Fannie a sympathetic smile. "Thanks for trying. Don't worry so. The team will carry on without you."

"Will they?"

The girls were all younger than Fannie was. They didn't believe in the project the way she did. They weren't beholden to Connie the way she was. If Connie had to sell her property, Fannie would lose more than a friend. She'd lose the job she loved. Riding and training horses was more than a childish pastime. It was what Fannie wanted to do for the rest of her life.

Fannie's Amish upbringing put her squarely at odds with her dream. Although some unmarried Amish women ran their own businesses, it wasn't common. Some worked for English employers but only until they chose to be baptized. Most worked in their family's businesses. Her parents and the bishop wouldn't approve of her riding once she was baptized, she was sure of that. Unless she chose to give up her Amish faith, it was unlikely she could follow her dream.

Could she leave behind all she had been raised to believe in? She wasn't ready to make that decision. Not yet.

"I think the team will do fine," Connie said, but she didn't sound sure.

Fannie pushed her uncertainty aside to concentrate on her friend. "I wanted to do this for you. I owe you so much."

Connie continued to brush her horse. "You have to get over thinking I did something special, Fannie. I didn't."

"You kept me from making the biggest mistake of my life. That was something special."

"It was your love of horses that led you to make the right decision. I only wish those other young people had made the same choice."

"So do I." Fannie cringed inwardly as she thought about the night that had ended so tragically less than two months after her seventeenth birthday.

"Have you settled on the number of patterns the girls will perform?" Connie clearly wanted to change the subject, and Fannie let her.

"Not yet, but I will before I leave. Have you had any inquiries from the ad you ran on the Horse and Tack website?"

"Lowball bids, nothing serious. Maybe I'm just a poor marketer. These horses should sell themselves. If I had the money, I'd have a professional video made. That might do the trick."

"My father says the *Englisch* want an angle, a story. A good horse for sale isn't enough. It has to be an Amish-raised and Amish-trained horse. That's okay for him, but it doesn't help you."

"I can always say raised near the Amish and trained as the Amish would, but that lacks punch even if it is accurate."

Fannie shook her head and realized her *kapp* was missing. *Mamm* would be upset with her for losing another one. She pulled a white handkerchief from her pocket. She always carried two for just this reason. She folded it into a triangle and tied it at the nape of her neck.

A woman should cover her head when she prayed, and Fannie was in serious need of prayers.

She couldn't believe it was part of God's plan for her to abandon her friend and to leave her beloved horses behind. "It amazes me how the *Englisch* think anything Amish must be better. We are the same as everyone else."

"You're right. There are good, hardworking people everywhere. If only hard work were enough to keep this place going. I'm glad my father isn't here to see how I've run it into the ground."

"You took care of your father as well as any daughter could. It wasn't possible to grow the business while he was so ill. You had a mountain of your father's medical bills to pay and you have done that. You will get this place back to the way it was and even better."

Fannie followed Connie's gaze as she glanced around the farm. Only four of the twelve stalls in the long, narrow barn were being used by boarders. The barn was beginning to show signs of wear and tear. The red paint was faded and peeling in places. Cobwebs hung from the rafters. A soggy spot at the end of the alley showed where the roof leaked, but all the Haflinger horses in the paddock and pasture were well cared for, with shining coats that gleamed golden brown in the sunshine. Connie took excellent care of her animals.

Attached to the barn was an indoor riding area where Connie's nine-year-old daughter, Zoe, was practicing her trick-riding moves on her Haflinger mare. Connie had once crisscrossed the United States performing at rodeos and equestrian events as a trick rider herself. She paused in her work to watch her daughter.

"I have got to make a go here, Fannie. I have to leave my daughter something besides tarnished belt buckles, fading ribbons and debts. I don't want to sell any of this land. My father made me promise that I wouldn't and I want to honor his wishes. After I'm gone, Zoe will be free to sell or stay. That will be my gift to her. A woman should be able to choose her own path in life."

"I couldn't agree with you more."

Connie shot her a puzzled glance. "Strange words coming from an Amish lass. I thought an Amish woman's goal in life was to be a wife and a mother."

"It is for most of the women, but I can't imagine being so tied down. I certainly don't want to marry and give some oaf the right to boss me around." To give up riding horses was like asking her to give up part of her soul.

"Does that mean you are thinking about leaving the Amish? I know some young people do, but won't you be shunned if you decide to leave?"

"My church believes each person must make that choice. If I leave before I am baptized into the faith, I won't be punished, but I know my parents won't allow me to continue staying at home. If I do decide not to be baptized, I was hoping I could work for you full-time and get my own place someday."

"If your plan with the drill team works out, I sure would consider taking you on full-time. I've never seen anyone as good with horses as you are. But don't give up on the idea of marriage. I can't see you settling for an oaf. It will take a special fellow to get harnessed to you, but I think he exists and I can't wait to meet him."

"I don't think he exists and I'm sure not going to waste my time looking for him."

"If I'd had that attitude before I met Zack, I wouldn't have Zoe now. It was a fair trade. Look at that girl go. She is fearless." Maternal pride glowed on her face as she watched her daughter circling the arena on her horse.

"She's really getting good," Fannie said. Trick riding was something she had always wanted to try.

"Better than I was at her age. I shouldn't encourage her, but I can't help it. The girl is like a sponge. She soaks in everything I tell her. I guess I'm one of those mothers who relive their glory days through their kids."

"Do you miss it?"

Connie paused in her work. "Sometimes I do, but that life is behind me along with my failed marriage to Zoe's father. Dad's illness was the excuse I used to come home, but that wasn't the whole truth. I missed staying in one place. Zack was the one with a restless spirit. Besides, I didn't want Zoe to grow up in a camper, always headed down the road to the next rodeo. I wanted her to have a home—a real home—and Dad gave us that."

She cupped her hands around her mouth. "Point your toes down, Zoe. Keep those legs straight and arch your back more."

"Like this?" Zoe shouted.

"That's better. That's a pretty good hippodrome stand."

Zoe grinned and waved one hand in acknowledgment as she stood atop the back of a gently loping golden horse with a wide white blaze down its face.

"Zoe is going to miss you," Connie said, turning back to Fannie.

"Don't give up on me yet. I may still find a way to stay." Fannie had no idea what that would be, but she wouldn't stop trying.

Connie put down her brush and motioned toward a pitchfork leaning against the wall. "Good. Until then, you still have work to do. I don't pay you much, but I expect you to earn it."

Fannie laughed as she picked up the fork. "I

would exercise your horses for free, but cleaning stalls will still cost you."

Connie untied the lead ropes of both horses. "I'll put these two away. You start on stall five and work your way down. George should be here soon. That man is always late. I wish I hadn't hired him."

George was another part-time stable hand at the farm. Connie insisted she couldn't afford full-time help, but in Fannie's eyes, George wasn't worth even part-time wages. He spent most of his time flirting with the girls in Fannie's riding group—or any woman who came to the farm.

Connie motioned toward her daughter. "I'll be back after I help Zoe with her technique. She's getting flat-footed again and that's dangerous, even on Misty."

Fannie set to work in the stall Connie had indicated, but her mind wasn't on the tasks before her. She still had to find a way to convince her parents that Betsy was the one they needed to send to Florida. No amount of pleading by her and her sister had changed their mother's mind so far. Their father might be persuaded, but their mother was adamant.

If only Noah had agreed to her plan. She wanted to be angry with him, but she couldn't. He was right. Her idea bordered on being dishonest, even if it was for a good cause. She didn't want to be courted by anyone, but having Noah reject her outright was humiliating. She wasn't that ugly, was she? There had been a time when she liked him—a lot. She tossed a forkful of straw into the wheelbarrow at her side.

She had liked being kissed by him, too. A lot. Jabbing the fork into the pile of dirty straw, she tried to forget about that night. She was the *dummkopf* for dumping her drink on him. He sure wouldn't try that again.

"Fannie, can I talk to you?"

She shrieked and spun around at the sound of Noah's voice, sending her forkful of dirty straw flying in his direction.

Chapter Three

Noah stared at the debris clinging to his navy blue ball-uniform pants and white socks. "Remind me to make sure you have empty hands before I speak to you in the future."

He looked up to see Fannie's shocked expression change to a guarded one. "Why are you here? Was there some insult you forgot to offer?"

"My first instinct is to say I'm saving one for another day, but I'm actually here to apologize and to hear you out."

Her eyes narrowed. "Are you saying you'll help me?"

He brushed down the front of his pants. Was he really going to go through with this? "Are you going to keep throwing things at me?"

"That was an accident."

"Accidents seem to happen around you often."

At least, it seemed that way to him, as he'd been on the receiving end of them more than once.

She folded her arms over her chest. "I thought you were going to apologize."

Time to get on with it. "Fannie, please accept my apology for calling you crazy."

"All right. I forgive you."

"*Danki.* Now it's your turn."

She thrust out her chin. "For what?"

"For calling me a *dummkopf.*"

"Lots of Amish folks have nicknames. That's mine for you."

He threw his hands in the air. "What am I even doing here?"

She reached out and caught hold of his arm. "I'm sorry. Please forgive me for calling you names. Will you help me?"

"I think a courtship—a pretend courtship— could be in my best interest as well as yours."

She squealed. "Noah, I could hug you right now."

He held out both hands. "Drop the pitchfork first."

She laughed softly, a bright, happy sound he discovered he liked. Leaning the implement against the wall, she turned back to him. "What made you change your mind?"

"You were right about *Mamm*'s plans for my summer. How did you know?"

"Rebecca, Mary and Lillian were talking about it at the quilting bee last week."

That the three of his sisters-in-law were in on it didn't surprise him. Wedded bliss was catching in his family. He started picking the loose straw from his socks. "What were you doing at the quilting bee?"

"Quilting. We were making a wedding gift for my cousin. Caring for horses isn't all I know how to do." She offered him a handkerchief from her pocket.

He used it to wipe his hands. "I didn't mean it that way."

"I can cook, clean, sew and manage a house. I just prefer taking care of horses."

"I don't blame you. *Mamm* made all her sons learn to cook, in case we had to take care of ourselves again. I learned, but I never liked it. Actually, Timothy is a good cook. Samuel, Joshua and I can get by, but Luke can't boil water."

He was stalling, trying to decide if he was making the right decision. Going out with Fannie wouldn't be that bad, would it? He liked horses almost as much as she did. That would give them something to talk about. How would she feel about his playing ball all summer? She said she wasn't ready to settle down, and he believed her, but what if she changed her mind after going out with him? He didn't mind teasing her, but he didn't want to hurt her feelings if she fell for him.

She tipped her head to the side. "When did you and your brothers have to take care of yourselves?"

He realized she didn't know the story. He launched into it with relief. Anything to delay the moment.

"When I was two, my mother became very ill. So ill that my father feared for her life. The way she tells it, there was a terrible blizzard. Rather than risk taking all of us out in the storm, *Daed* left Samuel in charge, bundled my mother in all the quilts we could spare and set out for the doctor's office in town. The doctor was able to get mother to the hospital, but the storm was so bad that *Daed* couldn't get back. Samuel took care of us and all the farm animals for three days until the blizzard let up. All we had to eat for those three days was bread soaked in milk with honey, because Samuel didn't know how to cook anything."

"How old was he?"

"If I was two, he would have been ten."

"By the time I was ten I could cook almost anything—fried chicken, baked ham."

"How is your bread?"

She folded her arms over her chest. "I make *goot* bread."

"And your cakes?"

"Light as a feather angel food, or do you prefer dense, gooey shoofly pie?"

"Shoofly, hands down. What about your egg noodles?"

"They could be better but they won't choke you. Why all the questions about my cooking?"

He took a deep breath. "My *daed* always said a man should never date a woman he wouldn't marry. I'll never marry a bad cook, so I won't date one."

She clasped her hands together. "So you *are* going to walk out with me?"

He rubbed his damp palms on his pants. "I want you to know that I'll be playing ball a lot this summer. You might miss some parties and such because I won't be able to take you."

"That's okay. I'm not much of a party person. Besides, I'll be busy with my equestrian team. But we will have to see each other often enough to convince my parents we are dating."

"Okay. I guess I'm in."

She jumped at him and gave him a quick hug before he could stop her. Then she flew out of the stall calling back, "I have to tell Connie."

What had he gotten himself into? Would a summer of being paraded before unknown and hopeful women be worse than a summer of Fannie?

It would, because his parents would make sure

he stopped playing ball. He couldn't let that happen. His friends were depending on him and he needed to know if he was good enough to become a professional player. God would decide, but Noah knew he'd have to do the work.

Fannie rushed back into the stall a few seconds later. "*Danki*, Noah. You have no idea how much this means to me."

"We are helping each other. I think."

Moving to stand in front of him, she gazed into his eyes. "If you truly feel this is wrong, Noah, you shouldn't do it. I'll find another way."

"It isn't exactly honest, but we aren't hurting anyone. I've walked out with a few girls and it never led to marriage. There's no reason I can't take you home from church a few times or to a party to see if we would suit."

She drew back. "We won't. I'm sure of it. You are not the man I want to marry."

"*Goot* to know. I was worried."

"Don't be. By the end of August, I'll be ready to take Betsy's place in Florida if she wants to come home. You're right, we aren't hurting anyone. Betsy wants to go in my place. She is much better at caring for the elderly than I am, and our grandparents deserve the best."

"I see your point there."

"Do you? Connie does need my help, too. You

can see that for yourself. This place will soon be on its last legs."

"That's no lie," George Milton said from the doorway. A handsome man with dark hair and dark eyes, George was an English fellow a couple of years younger than Noah. Noah knew him only slightly.

"This is a private conversation, George." Fannie leveled a sour look at him.

"Excuse me!" He rolled his eyes and walked on.

"You don't care for him?" Noah asked. He didn't, either.

"He is sloppy in his work. As I was saying, I'll enjoy riding on the drill team enormously, I won't lie about that, but I can and will be as much help to my mother as Betsy would be. Plus, I can still help my father with his horses. I'm willing to work hard and see that no one suffers because of this decision."

Noah's conscience pricked him. Fannie's reasons for this pretend courtship were more self-less than his. He simply wanted to keep playing ball.

Her face brightened. "I won't make demands on your time, Noah. If you happen to like one of the women coming to visit, I'll step aside and give you free rein."

He managed a half smile. "A fella isn't likely to get such a generous offer from a normal girlfriend."

She slapped his shoulder. "Well, you are a fortunate fellow, Noah Bowman. I'm not an ordinary girlfriend."

With a toss of her pretty head that reminded him of her spirited mare, Fannie walked out of the stall with a sassy stride that drew his attention to her trim figure. Among the earthy and familiar smells of the stable, he caught a whiff of something flowery.

Nope, there was nothing ordinary about Fannie.

Realizing he'd forgotten to give her the *kapp* she had dropped, he pulled it from his pocket and lifted it to his nose. A scent that reminded him of his mother's flower garden in summer clung to the fabric. Since Amish women didn't use perfume, he knew the smell must be from the shampoo Fannie used.

Flowery and sweet. Not what he expected from a girl who spent most of her time with horses.

He walked out into the arena and saw her with a half-dozen other Amish girls. They were saddling Connie's horses. All of the girls eyed him intently as Fannie left them to speak to him. "The rest of my team is here. Do you want to watch us practice?"

"Another time. Walter is waiting outside to drive us to our game in Berlin. Do they all know about us?" He jerked his head toward the girls.

"Only Connie knows."

He squared his shoulders and held out Fannie's *kapp*. "That's a relief. I guess I should get this over with. Fannie, may I take you home after church tomorrow?"

She glanced over her shoulder and then leaned close. "If you have to grit your teeth to ask me out, Noah, no one will believe we like each other."

His mouth fell open. He snapped it shut and glared at her. "That is exactly what I said. *Ja* or *nee*, Fannie. Can I take you home after church or not? I don't have all day."

Her sweet smile didn't reach her eyes. "As much as I would like to refuse your kind offer, I won't. I will almost be happy to go out with you."

He crossed his arms over his chest. "And I will be sincerely happy when this charade is over."

She took a step closer and whispered, "Not nearly as happy as I will be."

"You ungrateful minx. Enjoy your time in Florida." He turned away.

She caught his arm before he had taken a single step. "I'm sorry, Noah. Really. Please don't go away mad. I will do better."

"I must be *ab en kopp*, off in the head. Otherwise, why would I be here?"

She looked over her shoulder and then turned to him with resignation written across her face. "You're right. No one will believe we are a couple. I'm not as pretty as the girls you've gone out with in the past. I'm much too horsey for most men to look my way. I don't know how to act around a fella who shows some interest, so I act as if I don't care. You've been a friend to me in the past and I hope that we can be friends again in the future. I'm sorry I put you in an awkward situation."

If she had been a motherless kitten, she couldn't have looked more forlorn. It was too bad he had a soft spot for kittens. He looked toward the group of young women watching them and sighed heavily. "Fannie, we might not be friends after this, but your teammates are gonna believe we're a couple."

Calling himself every kind of fool, he took her by the shoulders, pulled her close and kissed her cheek. Then he beat a hasty retreat before she had time to react.

Fannie pressed a hand to her tingling face. Had Noah wanted to kiss her, or had he done it purely for effect?

For the effect, the sensible part of her insisted.

The less sensible part of her wondered if he liked her—just a little. She stared at the door where he'd disappeared until the sound of giggling and a wolf whistle penetrated the fog in her mind.

She turned to face her teammates, ignoring George's leering stare from across the arena. "We have a lot of work to do and only a short time to do it. Mount up. Zoe, start the music."

Connie came over and handed Fannie Trinket's reins as the strains of "She'll Be Coming 'Round the Mountain" blared from a speaker on the arena railing. The group had decided on the song because the rolling cadence of the music matched the gait of their horses.

Connie held on to Trinket's reins as she gazed at Fannie's face. "Just remember that people who play with fire often get burned."

"I'm not going to get burned," Fannie said quietly, praying that was true. "I know the difference between real and pretend."

"For your sake, I hope so."

Every time Fannie looked up from her hymnal on Sunday morning, she caught sight of Noah's reflection in the mirror on the wall behind the bishop and preachers at the front of the room, and she started thinking about Noah's kiss all over again.

The service was being held at the home of John

Miller, the local blacksmith. The widower lived with his mother on a small farm a mile from Fannie's home. Like many Amish homes, the walls of the downstairs could be opened up to accommodate members of the congregation during services that were held every other Sunday. Wooden benches had been placed in two rows where women sat on one side while the men sat on the other.

She should be minding the words of the bishop's preaching, but all Fannie could think about was riding home with Noah that evening. After the singing that would be held for the youth following supper. After dark.

Would he kiss her again?

She gave herself a mental shake. The whole idea was ridiculous. How could she pretend to be interested in Noah when she wasn't? The longer she thought about it, and she'd spent most of the night thinking about it, the less she wanted to go through with it. The only answer was to call the whole thing off.

She couldn't silence the talk among the girls who'd seen him kiss her, but it would die down and none of them were likely to spread the story if Noah didn't come around again. George would forget about it soon enough, and he knew very few Amish folk.

Calling it off was the right decision. She would tell Noah as soon as she had the chance.

She glanced at the mirror again. She could see a half dozen of the young unmarried men and boys in the reflection. They were all seated at the back of the room nearest the door. They would be the first to leave when the three-hour service was over. Several of them drew frowns from the ministers by their restlessness as the end approached. Fannie couldn't blame them. The backless wooden benches were hard. She focused again on the heavy black songbook in her hands. She had been desperate, and her spur-of-the-moment plan had been foolish. There had to be a better way. If only she could think of one.

"Why is Noah Bowman watching you?" Betsy whispered in her ear.

Fannie glanced up and met Noah's eyes in the mirror. He nodded slightly to acknowledge her. A rush of heat filled her cheeks and she looked down quickly. "I have no idea."

"*Shveshtah*, you're blushing." Betsy smirked, causing several nearby worshippers to look their way.

Fannie shot her sister a fierce stare and Betsy turned her attention back to the bishop. Fannie glanced in the mirror again.

Unlike yesterday, Noah was dressed plain in

black pants and a black coat over a pale blue shirt. He was indistinguishable from the other Amish men around him except for the shorter haircut he wore. He wasn't the most handsome one of the Bowman brothers. Luke was the best looking while Samuel was the most hardworking, but Noah was nice looking in his own way. She liked his eyes the best. Her sister called them forget-me-not blue. Fannie liked the way they sparkled when he smiled. And he was almost always smiling.

Except when he was around her.

Not that she smiled that much around him, either. Ever since that evening in his mother's garden, they seemed to rub each other the wrong way. Fannie couldn't put her finger on the reason.

People around her began singing and Fannie joined in, knowing it was the final hymn of the service. Normally the preaching seemed long, but not today. Today it ended all too quickly. When she walked outside, Noah was waiting for her off to the side of the house with his straw hat in his hands. She clutched her fingers together and walked toward him.

"You look like a martyr heading to your own execution. Try smiling." He nodded to someone behind her.

Fannie swallowed the comment that sprang to her lips and smiled instead. "Is this better?"

"*Vennich.*"

"A little is better than nothing." She looked over her shoulder and saw his mother smiling warmly at them. Anna winked at her and waved before snagging Fannie's mother by the arm, and the two of them walked away with their heads close together.

Fannie kept her grin in place with difficulty as she turned back to Noah. "You didn't tell your mother we were going out, did you?"

He gave her a sheepish look and shrugged. "I kind of did."

Fannie pointed to their mothers as they stood talking to each other. "She's going to tell my mother, and I haven't mentioned it to her."

"*Mamm* put me on the spot."

"In what way?"

He grabbed Fannie's arm and led her around the side of the building. "She said I had to end my *rumspringa* and look for a wife this summer. She meant it, so I told her I was already seeing you. This is what you wanted, isn't it? This was your idea."

Why hadn't she thought this through before rushing over to see Noah? "I was thinking my mother was the only one who needed to believe we were going out. I didn't consider how your mother would feel about it."

"She's thrilled. Very, very thrilled."

Fannie closed her eyes and cringed. "Of course she is. She and my mother are the best of friends. How are we going to break it to them that we aren't getting married?"

"Whoa. Slow down, Fannie. Don't get ahead of yourself. We haven't had a date yet. Let's stick to the plan at least until the second week of August."

That was the weekend of the Horse Expo, but he didn't know that. "Why then?"

"The state invitational baseball tournament is being held that weekend."

She took a step away from him. "Wait a minute. You told your mother we were going out so you could keep playing baseball this summer?"

"Don't take that tone with me. I have my reasons for agreeing to this just like you had your reasons for coming up with this idea."

And to think she had been wondering if he liked her even a little. "It'll never work. I'm sorry I ever suggested it."

"Don't be hasty. I'm willing to give it a try, unless you have your heart set on leaving for Florida next week."

She folded her arms across her middle. How could she tell Connie she'd changed her mind after assuring her friend she would help her? She couldn't. "It looks like you and I are stuck with each other for the summer. Very well. What are your plans for our first date?"

"We do what normal people do. We'll stay for the singing tonight and I'll take you home afterward."

"Don't expect an invitation to come in and visit, the way normal couples do."

"If I get home too early, my parents are going to think we didn't hit it off."

"So drive around for an hour or two."

"I'm not wearing out a good horse just to make you happy."

"You wouldn't know a good horse if you tripped over one."

"How can you, of all people, say that?"

She opened her mouth to reply, but his brother Joshua came around the corner of the building. "Here you are. It's our turn to go in and eat, Noah."

"*Danki*, I'm coming."

Joshua smiled at Fannie. "Would you care to join Mary and Hannah when they go in? I know they would enjoy visiting with you."

"*Danki*, Joshua, but I have to find my sister."

"We are getting up a game of horseshoes after lunch. Noah and I will take on you and your sister, won't we, *bruder*?" Joshua seemed intent on getting her together with the rest of Noah's family. Had Noah's mother told them all that she and Noah were dating?

She forced a bright smile for Noah. "I'd love the chance to beat Noah at any game of his choosing."

Joshua laughed. "Well, don't pick baseball. Did he tell you he pitched a no-hitter yesterday? Against the league champions from last year. Everyone at the fire station thinks this year's trophy will look awesome on our wall. The boy has an amazing arm."

Fannie was surprised when Joshua winked at her, too. "I'm glad he's finally showing some sense in his personal life."

She wanted to sink into the ground.

Joshua left when he heard the sound of his wife's voice calling him, but Noah lingered.

Fannie's temper cooled rapidly. "I'm sorry."

"Don't worry about it. We seem to be trapped by our little deception. Do we tell them now or let them down gradually?"

"Gradually, I guess. We started this so we might as well finish it. The next time I have a brilliant idea, don't listen to me."

"I won't."

She stared at her feet for a long moment. "A no-hitter. Wow, that's quite an accomplishment."

"It was due more to great fielding by the team than my pitching. *Gott* smiled on us."

She was glad to hear him giving credit to others and to God. The awkward silence grew between them. Finally, she said, "I do need to find my sister."

"Sure. See you later at the horseshoe pit."

"Okay."

"Don't think I'll take it easy on you," he said as he walked away.

"The thought never crossed my mind, but you'd better not."

A small grin curved his lips. There was a distinct twinkle in his eyes. "You won't knock me in the head with a horseshoe, will you?"

"I have already promised to stop throwing things at you."

"*Goot.* I'll hold you to that." His grin turned to a wide smile just before he rounded the corner.

Fannie leaned back against the wall of the house as a funny feeling settled in the center of her stomach. He sure was an attractive fellow when he smiled.

She shook her head at her own foolishness. "I'm not going to fall for him. This was definitely my worst idea yet."

It would be difficult to guard her emotions if she had to spend much time in his company. If he was being nice to her, she wasn't sure she could do it.

Chapter Four

"I'm glad that's over with." Noah held out his hand to help Fannie into his open buggy after the singing that evening.

"So am I." Fannie ignored his hand and climbed in by herself. "Did you see everyone staring at me when I first came in? I almost turned and ran."

"Now that you mention it, I can't think of the last time I saw you at a young people's gathering."

"They're a waste of time if you aren't shopping for a potential spouse."

"Not everyone is looking to marry. A lot of us just want to have fun."

"The boys are there for fun. The girls are all looking for someone to marry. I noticed plenty of them eyeing you. Especially the bishop's visiting nieces. In the future, could you at least act as if you are interested in me?"

"Maybe I'm not that good of an actor," he snapped.

"Work on it or this will be pointless." She scooted as far away from him as she could get without falling out the other side of his buggy.

She was right to rebuke him. He had neglected her, but a group of his friends had wanted to talk baseball. He got caught up in the conversation until it was almost time to go home. That's when he noticed Fannie sitting beside her sister and her sister's beau, and recalled why she was there. He'd spent the last half hour sitting beside Fannie but mostly talking to Hiram as Fannie fumed. He knew the buggy ride home was going to be a rough one.

Deciding he should smooth the troubled waters with a compliment or two, he climbed in beside her. "I noticed during the singing tonight that *Gott* has given you a fine voice."

"*Danki.* You have a pleasant voice, too." She stared straight ahead with her arms clasped tight across her middle. Was she nervous? It wasn't as if it was a real date.

"You don't have to hang off the side. I don't bite."

"I do," she quipped, but she relented and inched a little closer.

"Do you want to drive?" He offered her the reins.

She looked at him then. "Why?"

"I'm just asking. I know you're almost as good a driver as I am."

She sat up straight and planted her hands on her hips. "*Almost* as good?"

He flinched at her offended tone. That had been the wrong choice of words. So much for smoother waters. "Do you want to drive or not?"

"All right." She accepted the reins and neatly turned Willy to head out of John Miller's yard. It was after ten o'clock, and the other couples and singles were already gone.

Noah propped his feet on the dash rail and crossed his hands behind his head. "Willy has a tendency to drift to the left."

"I see that." She corrected the horse's line and stopped him at the highway, where John Miller's lane intersected it at the top of a steep hill. When she was sure the way was clear, she eased Willy out onto the blacktop.

At the bottom of the hill, a hundred yards away, the road ended in a T. Beyond the roadway the tree-lined river slipped silently through the farmland. Fannie turned Willy onto the road that skirted the riverbank. Breaks in the trees occasionally gave Noah a glimpse of moonlight rippling on the water's surface.

He studied Fannie's face as she sat beside him. A soft wind fluttered the ribbons of her *kapp* and tugged at the curls she tried so hard to confine. She held the reins with confidence, as he knew she would. He'd seen her helping her father train horses to pull buggies since she was knee-high. "Nice night for a drive."

"I reckon. Driving at night makes me nervous."

So the unflappable Fannie had a weakness. "Why?"

"I'm always afraid a car will come up behind me too fast and run into me."

"It happens. We can't know when *Gott* will test our faith with such a trial. Do you want me to take over?"

"*Nee.* I must overcome this fear."

He worried about the tremor in her voice. She really was scared—but determined. "What do you think of Willy?" he asked, to take her mind off her apprehension.

"He's a sweet goer. Nice smooth gait. A high stepper but not absurdly high. He has a soft mouth and responds to a light touch on the reins. He's a *goot gaul.*"

"And you said I wouldn't know a good horse if I tripped over one."

She sent him a sidelong glance, but seemed to consider her words for a change. "Sometimes my mouth says things before my brain can stop it. Forgive me."

An olive branch? He gladly accepted it. "You are forgiven. I've been known to speak rashly, too."

"Sadly, that seems to be all we have in common."

"We both like horses."

A hint of a smile lifted one corner of her mouth. "There is that."

"I'm sure we'll find other things we can agree on by the end of the month. I'll try if you will."

"I reckon there's no harm in trying. At least you aren't as boring as Hiram. I don't know how my sister stands him."

"It might be uncharitable of me, but I have to agree. He is a boring fellow. If you don't love pigs, there's no point in striking up a conversation with him."

She giggled and Noah relaxed. The drive wasn't so bad after that. It wasn't long before the fence that marked her lane came into view up ahead. She turned Willy neatly into her driveway and pulled him to a stop in front of her house. The building was dark except for a dim light glowing in the kitchen window.

She handed Noah the reins. "Would you like to come in?"

"I thought you weren't going to ask me in."

"Another one of my mouth-before-brain moments."

It was an accepted custom for an Amish girl to

invite her date in for a visit, even though her parents would be in bed. The young man and woman were expected to be on their best behavior. They would talk or play board games until very late as they got to know each other.

"I don't see Hiram's buggy. Do you think he's gone home already? I know he left with your sister."

"He never stays long."

Noah shrugged. "He's an odd duck. Sure, I'd like to come in."

"Really?" The look of shock on her face was priceless.

He hopped down, secured Willy and turned to help Fannie out of the buggy, but she was already standing on the ground. "You don't have to come in, Noah. We can pretend you did."

"I think we've done enough pretending for a while, don't you?"

"I reckon you're right."

She led the way inside and closed the door quietly behind him. "I made some cinnamon-raisin biscuits this morning. Would you like one?"

"Sounds *goot*."

"Do you want to sit in the living room or here in the kitchen?" She had her hands clenched tightly together.

"The normal place for a couple to visit is in

the living room, but I like the kitchen better. It's cozy." He took a seat at the table.

She seemed to relax. "I agree. No point in trying for a normal courtship at this point."

Moving to the cupboard, she removed two plates and placed two biscuits on his and one on hers. She sat down at the table and pushed his plate toward him. He wasn't hungry, but he pulled off a small piece and ate it. The raisins were plump but the dough was tough.

"How is it?" she asked.

"It won't choke me."

She scowled and opened her mouth but he forestalled her. "Brain first, mouth second, Fannie."

Her scowl faded and she blushed. "They aren't my best."

"They're far better than anything I could make. I imagine cooking is like playing ball. It takes a lot of practice to get good enough to make it look easy."

"Do you practice your pitching at home?"

"Some. I have to pester my brothers or my cousins to catch for me. They don't always have time."

"Have you always liked playing ball?"

"Are you kidding? What boy doesn't? Don't you remember all the recesses we spent playing softball at school?"

"I remember staying in to write I'm sorry for

something or other on the blackboard a hundred times. I was always in trouble. I wasn't any good at hitting the ball so I wasn't picked for a team very often."

"I used to get you in trouble a lot. I thought it was funny to see you get angry. Your face got so red. I'm sorry about that."

She shrugged. "We were kids."

"Still. It wasn't kind of me."

They talked about school for a while, sharing memories and funny stories from their childhood days. It surprised Noah that she recalled so many of his exploits. The Bowman boys were known for their adventuresome natures, but he wasn't the wildest one.

"Luke was the worst of us," Noah admitted. His brother had left the Amish and gotten into trouble with the English law over drugs, bringing shame to the family.

Fannie's eyes filled with sympathy. "No one would know it now. He's changed for the better."

"*Gott* and Emma changed his heart." Luke had become a devout member of the faithful, much to his family's joy.

"Does your brother Timothy like teaching school? It's unusual for a man to become a teacher." She nibbled on the edge of her biscuit.

"He loves it, especially since his wife, Lillian, teaches there, as well. You heard the school is holding a frolic, didn't you? The school board has decided to add a wing to the building for the upper classes that Timothy teaches. They are pouring the new foundation next week."

"We heard about it. *Mamm* and *Daed* have said they will help."

"That's great. The more hands we have, the easier the work will be."

She sighed heavily. "It's odd to think about our school changing as much as it has."

"You haven't said you forgive me for teasing you the way I did back then."

"I forgive you." She looked at him from under lowered brows. "Just don't do it again."

He chuckled. "If you don't throw stuff at me, I won't call you carrottop, copperhead, fire-eater or ginger nut ever again."

"Aw, thanks for nothing. Ginger nut? No one ever called me a ginger nut."

"Did I miss that one when we were young?"

She plucked a raisin from her biscuit and tossed it toward him. He caught it in his open mouth and she giggled.

He sat up straighter. "I say you can't do that again."

"And I say I'm not going to spend time sweeping the kitchen floor after my failures. Besides, I think it's time you went home."

He checked the clock on the wall, surprised to

see how late it was. "I reckon you're right. Our team has a game next Saturday. Would you care to come and watch?"

"I can't. We have our first competition at the Wayne's County Fairgrounds that day. That's if I'm not on my way to Florida. You can come watch us practice at Connie's place on Tuesdays and Thursdays at six."

"Are you sure I won't be bored?"

"I doubt it. You appreciate good horses the same way I do."

"I'm thinking not as much as you do. Our team, the Fire Eaters, practice on Wednesdays and Fridays at five o'clock over behind the fire station. You're welcome to come watch us."

She wrinkled her nose and shook her head. "Talk about boring."

"Do I sense disdain for the sport I love?"

"I think it's silly to see grown men acting like little boys throwing a ball at each other and trying to hit it with a stick."

He scowled at her. "Is it sillier than a bunch of girls riding their horses in circles?"

She rose and folded her arms across her middle. "I think it is."

He pressed his lips together and settled his straw hat on his head. "I don't have a comeback for that. It is time I went home."

"Don't worry. I'm sure you'll think of the perfect thing to say before you get across the road."

"Now you imply my wit is slow." He shook his head, moved to the door and jerked it open. "What have I done to deserve this?"

"I won't begin the litany of your sins, Noah Bowman. It would take me the rest of the night to list them." Her face was expressionless as she slammed the door behind him.

Noah felt like banging his head on it. Ten minutes ago he'd been enjoying himself and thinking Fannie had certainly grown into an interesting woman. In the blink of an eye she was back to insulting him like a schoolgirl.

He walked to his buggy and untied Willy from the hitching rail in front of her house. "This is proof the whole thing is a bad idea, but now I'm stuck with it."

He'd do well to think of this courtship as a business deal, one that got them what they both wanted, but it was sure going to be a painful summer.

"Anna Bowman tells me you and Noah have been seeing each other. Is this so?" Fannie's mother asked, once they were alone the next morning.

Fannie swept the breakfast crumbs from the

table and tossed them in the trash before answering. "We've been out together."

"I thought it was odd that you wanted to stay for the singing yesterday. Did he bring you home last night?"

"If you must know, he did."

"Well? How is it going?"

"Better than I expected."

That was the truth. Fannie couldn't believe how much she had enjoyed sitting alone with him in the kitchen and just talking. It was as if they had both put aside the masks they wore in daily life. Until she insulted him. When would she learn to think before she spoke?

"So?" her mother prompted.

"So, what?"

"Child, you will drive me insane yet. Did he ask you out again?"

"Sort of. He invited me to come to his ball game on Saturday, but I'll be leaving so it doesn't matter."

"Of course it matters. I had no idea you and Noah were seeing each other. You should have said something sooner. Anna and I dreamed of seeing you two wed when you were still in diapers."

Fannie rolled her eyes. "We aren't getting married, *Mamm*. We've only started walking out together."

"But it was a nice date, *ja*?"

"*Ja*, it was nice, but he knows I'm leaving. I'm going to need new shoes before I head to Florida. Do you think we could go shopping tomorrow?" Fannie glanced at her mother from the corner of her eye. Was she wavering?

"Your sister has new shoes."

"Betsy doesn't wear the same size I do."

"I thought you wanted to stay here and ride horses with your friends."

"I do. It's important to me, but I realize you won't change your mind." Fannie wiped at a stubborn spot of dried jelly on the table. "If Noah is still unattached next year, maybe he'll ask me out again. Of course, his mother has invited a number of young women to visit them this summer, so I can't hold out a lot of hope."

Fannie's mother cupped one hand around her chin and tapped her lips with one finger. "Your sister is in the garden picking string beans. Ask her to come in."

"Okay." Fannie concealed a smile as she went out the door. Maybe, just maybe, her idea was going to bear fruit, after all.

At the garden gate, she called to Betsy. "*Mamm* wants to see you."

"What for?"

"I think she wants to ask you about going to Florida."

Betsy dashed to the gate carrying a blue plastic

bucket half-full of beans. "Really? That would be *wunderbar.*"

Fannie didn't want to hold out false hope. "She hasn't said for sure."

"I'll do my best to convince her." Betsy shoved her bucket into Fannie's hands and scampered through the gate. "You might as well get used to doing my chores. There's eight rows left to pick."

Fannie stared at the large garden loaded with produce that needed to be canned soon. Any free time she wanted would have to come after her work was done. She was going to have a busy summer. Opening the gate, she crossed to the beans and started picking where her sister had left off.

Entering the kitchen fifteen minutes later with a full pail, Fannie found her mother washing glass pint jars in the sink. The pressure cooker sat on the stove waiting to be loaded. Fannie fairly itched to hear her mother's decision, but instead of asking, she transferred a portion of her beans into a large bowl, rinsed them, sat down and began snapping them into equal lengths after discarding the stems.

Betsy came up from the cellar with a cardboard box full of dusty jars. She grinned at Fannie and nodded. She put the box on the counter beside her mother. Instead of jumping for joy,

Fannie kept snapping beans, but she couldn't hide her grin.

Her mother placed the last jar in soapy water to soak and turned around. After drying her hands on her apron, she smoothed her dress. "I must speak with your *daed*."

Fannie knew her father had the ultimate say in family matters, but he seldom went against his wife's wishes. As soon as her mother went out, Betsy flew to her sister and pulled her to her feet. She hugged Fannie and swung her around. "I'm going to see the ocean!"

"I'm glad you're happy about it."

"*Happy* is a poor word for this feeling." Holding Fannie at arm's length, Betsy stared at her with wide eyes. "How did you manage to change her mind?"

"Noah Bowman asked to walk out with me."

"I wondered who took you home from the singing. Noah Bowman? I never would have guessed. And that's all it took for *Mamm* to change her mind?"

"You know how desperate she is to see me wed."

"I do. Believe me, I do. I'm sure she thinks this is your last chance."

Fannie leaned back and frowned. "I wouldn't call it my last chance. I'm not even twenty-two."

"I've never seen anyone as determined to become an old maid as you are. You haven't had a date in years."

"Only because I wasn't willing to give up my free time. I'll date when I'm ready."

"Sure, if you say so. I don't care what the reason is. I'm going to Florida." Betsy threw her hands in the air and spun out of the room.

Fannie went out to gather more beans. Her mother was in the kitchen when she returned. She motioned for Fannie to join her at the table. "Sit for a moment. I have something to tell you."

Fannie took a seat and tried to keep her face blank.

Her mother steepled her fingers. "Your father and I have talked it over, and we believe Betsy should go to stay with my parents."

"She'll be happy to hear that, but what about Hiram?"

"They are betrothed now. That will not change if she is gone for a few months. I would feel terrible if I ruined your chances with Noah by sending you away."

Fannie tried hard to conceal her elation. "Is it still okay that I ride with the girls at Connie's place?"

"As long as your riding doesn't interfere with other things."

"It won't. I'll be as much help to you as I can, I promise."

"I was thinking of the time you might spend in Noah Bowman's company."

"He lives across the road. We'll see each other often enough."

"Men need prompting when it comes to courting, Fannie. You must make a good impression on him and show him you'll make a *goot* wife. Anna and I will arrange for the two of you to get together a few times a week."

Fannie shook her head. "*Mamm*, I'm not going to throw myself at Noah."

"I'm not asking you to do that. We're simply going to nudge him in the right direction. Your father says the boy has baseball practice at the fire station on Wednesday evening. You should go, and you should take all the men something sweet to eat."

"There are plenty of chores waiting for me. I don't have time to sit and watch Noah throw a ball."

Her mother scowled at her. "Most young women are thrilled at the idea of spending a little extra time with their beau. Are you saying you have already decided the two of you won't suit? If that's the case, there's no reason you can't go to Florida as we first decided."

"I'm not saying we won't suit," Fannie said quickly. "We've only gone out once. It's too soon to tell if we are meant for each other or not. Only *Gott* knows the one who will become my help-mate for life."

"This is true. Only *Gott* can bring forth the bounty of my garden out of the dirt, but I still have to pull the weeds and water the seedlings. A courtship is no different. You must do your part."

"I will, but you and Anna shouldn't interfere. Too much water can drown the seedlings."

Fannie's mother looked as if she wanted to argue, but to Fannie's surprise, she leaned back in her chair and said, "We will leave the courting to you *kinder*, but you must put some effort into the relationship. Anna will tell Noah the same. Going to watch him play ball is a start."

"We are hardly children, *Mamm*."

Her mother chuckled and cupped her hands around Fannie's face. "Both Anna and I are delighted that you two have found each other after all these years living right across the road from each other. Nothing could make us happier than seeing you and Noah wed. Just think, someday Anna and I could be sharing grandbabies."

Fannie swallowed hard against the sudden

tightness in her throat. How were she and Noah going to get out of this mess without hurting both their mothers?

Chapter Five

"Mamm, I don't think this is a good idea."

From inside their buggy, Fannie looked over the vehicles in the parking lot beside the fire station late on Wednesday afternoon. There were six buggies parked along the edge of the gravel lot. The rest were pickups, a motorcycle, several scooters, a few bicycles and two SUVs. Several dozen spectators, Amish and English men and women, sat in the bleachers behind the backstop. Four young Amish boys sat in the grass along the third base line. If she walked out to talk to Noah, the whole community would be speculating about their relationship before the next church meeting.

Fannie's mother made a shooing motion with her hand. "All men like to eat. Have faith in your mother. I snagged your father, didn't I? It was no easy task, but it was my cooking that did the trick. Now, go speak to Noah. I expect you home before dark."

Fannie got out of the buggy with a large hamper over her arm. Noah stood on the pitcher's mound facing a batter. He hadn't seen her yet. He leaned forward with the ball behind his back. He adjusted the brim of his ball cap, nodded once, checked the runners on second and third base and then threw a lightning-fast pitch. The umpire called a strike.

The ball field was a recent addition to the fire station grounds. The previous fall more than a dozen fires had been started in their community. Many Amish thought English teenagers were setting the blazes and distrust of the English ran high. When they learned the arsonist was an Amish person, the son of the school board president, everyone was shocked. In gratitude for the firemen's hard work, and to ease a few consciences, the men of the community improved a field behind the station from a cow pasture to a well-maintained ball diamond.

Fannie walked to the edge of the backstop. "Excuse me. May I speak with you?"

The umpire, the man she assumed was their coach, called a halt to the practice. He took off his face mask and she recognized Eric Swanson, the captain of the local fire department. "Is there something I can do for you, miss?"

"I have some snacks that I thought your players might enjoy."

He glanced at his watch. "That's real kind. We have about thirty minutes of practicing left. If you would like to leave them here, that would be fine."

Fannie was tempted to leave the hamper and scamper back to the buggy, but one look at her mother's face convinced her she needed to remain where she was. "Might I have a word with Noah first?"

The man frowned, but motioned for Noah to come in. "Take five, guys."

Noah trotted over to where she stood. "Fannie, what are you doing here? What's wrong?"

"Nothing's wrong. You invited me." She felt like a complete fool as the rest of the team and spectators stared at them.

Noah didn't look happy. "You didn't exactly express an interest in my invitation at the time."

"*Mamm* has changed my mind for me." Fannie looked over her shoulder in time to see her mother turn the buggy around and head toward home.

Noah shook his head. "I don't understand."

She lowered her voice to a whisper hoping they wouldn't be overheard. "I'm here to impress you with my baking skills and show you I'm interested in all that you do. According to my mother,

I have to put more effort into impressing you. Please act impressed instead of annoyed."

He frowned. "This is the reason you interrupted our practice?"

She glanced around at the people staring at them. "What did you imagine I would do when you invited me?"

"I don't know. Sit quietly on the sideline and watch."

"In other words, be meek and silent as a good Amish woman should."

"I don't know why I thought you could manage that."

"Noah, can this wait until later?" his coach asked.

"Sure," Noah said loudly before turning back to Fannie. "Thanks for coming, but I have to finish practicing."

He wasn't overjoyed to see her, but she'd expected as much. Pretending to enjoy someone's company was much harder than she thought it would be. "*Mamm* left me here, so you will have to take me home afterward."

"I can't. I have plans. Captain Swanson surprised us all with tickets to the Cleveland Indians game tonight and we'll barely make it if we leave here right after practice. I don't have time to take you home."

"What am I supposed to do?" she asked with a quick frown.

"It isn't that far for you to walk."

"Walk home alone?"

"Why don't you ask one of the other Amish guys to take you? I'm sure someone will. Ask the bishop's son, Rob Beachy, he's here. His cousin Simon plays shortstop for us."

It wasn't a long walk. Less than two miles but that wasn't the problem. "Arriving home alone will surely convince my mother you arc growing fonder of me by the hour. Letting the bishop's son take me home will convince her you are head over heels in love with me," Fannie said through gritted teeth, not holding back her sarcasm.

Noah's face hardened with displeasure as he leaned close. "I'm not going to miss a Cleveland game for the sake of a courtship that's not real."

"I don't imagine you'd miss that for a real courtship. Woe to the woman you pick to be your wife, Noah Bowman, that's all I can say. Enjoy the food. I hope it chokes you." She shoved the hamper into his hands and marched away. She wasn't about to sit and watch him practice his silly game.

Noah wanted to call Fannie back but thought better of it. There wasn't any point in trying to talk to her when she was upset. She could be the most stubborn, irritating and frustrating woman he'd ever met. It took her all of ten seconds to have him seeing red.

No, it wasn't all her fault. He'd spent an hour today listening to his mother sing Fannie's praises and offering him advice on courting her. He'd been ready to confess everything, except he knew what was at stake for both himself and Fannie. The deception didn't sit well with him, but he shouldn't have taken his sour mood out on her. She might have suggested the idea, but he was the one who jumped on the wagon when it looked like his plans for the summer were in jeopardy.

Eric Swanson came up beside him. "Noah, I don't normally make a point of getting involved in my player's personal lives, but may I give you some advice?"

"I reckon you will, no matter what I say." Eric was Noah's friend as well has his coach and captain of the fire department. He respected Eric opinion.

"I played for two years in the minors."

"For the Red Sox farm team. I know."

"In all that time, I rarely saw a pitcher with the kind of speed and control you have. I've been talking to people I know about you. Don't let something or someone distract you now, when we are so close to getting you in front of major-league scouts."

Noah shook his head. "I won't."

Fannie wouldn't become a distraction if he kept his head in the game.

"I'll see that he stays with the program," Walter said, joining them as he tossed the ball in the air and caught it.

Eric nodded once. "Good. Let's win the next four games and get this team to the state invitational. I understand you must have conflicted feelings, Noah. I'm not pressing you to make a decision you aren't ready to make. Just keep an open mind and give the team your all."

"I will." Noah smacked his fist into his glove.

"All right. Play ball," Eric yelled.

Walter smiled at Noah as he handed him the ball. "I respect your religious beliefs, too, and I understand if you choose to stay here, but I don't want to spend my life in Bowmans Crossing growing corn and milking cows with my dad. I never got to college, my folks didn't have the money for it, so I couldn't play college ball and get noticed that way. This could be my only shot at the pros. I'm not getting any younger, so keep your head in the game and not on a girl."

"It's not serious."

"I'm glad to hear that. Maybe a scout will pick both of us up for the same team. Wouldn't that be a hoot? You and me, pitching and catching in the major leagues. We'd put Bowmans Crossing on the map."

Noah walked back to the mound. He wasn't sure he wanted a life outside the Amish, but what if Eric was right? What if he *was* good enough? Didn't he deserve a chance to find out?

If he failed, he would know for certain it was because God wanted him here.

Noah left the blacksmith's shop on Thursday afternoon a little before six. He had come to consult with John Miller about a crack in Ginger's back hoof that his brother Joshua had discovered. John promised he would be over the next day to fit her with a special shoe to protect her foot from further injury. Noah had left her in a box stall to limit her movements until then.

At the bottom of the hill, Noah saw a young Amish girl cantering along the river's edge and wondered if she was headed to Connie Stroud's place. Today was the day Fannie told him that her group was practicing.

He hesitated as he wrestled with his conscience. He hadn't come this way with the intention of going on to Connie's farm, but he knew he should. He and Fannie had not parted on the best of terms the day before. She'd made an effort to come see him play ball. The least he could do in return was to watch the drill team that meant so much to her. It was a small olive branch but it was worth a try. The way things were going between them now, no one was going to believe they were courting seriously. He just hoped Fannie didn't run him off as soon as he poked his head into the barn.

Willy resisted slightly when Noah turned him away from home, but he was soon trotting along nicely. The rhythmic clatter of Willy's hooves on the pavement and the gentle creak and jingle of his harness were familiar sounds Noah had heard all his life. He could hear the birds in the trees along the river and the sound of the wind sighing through the branches. It was soothing to his troubled heart.

When a car roared around him and sped away, he spared a moment to pity the driver who was missing so much of God's beauty along this winding country road.

He turned into Connie's lane a mile and a half farther down the highway. White board fences lined both sides of the drive. On one side, golden Haflinger mares grazed peacefully while their frisky foals raced to the fence to gaze at Noah and whinny at the unfamiliar horse.

Half a dozen horses of assorted colors were tied to the hitching rail beside the barn. He tied Willy up beside them and walked into the riding arena.

Eight girls, including Fannie, were already mounted on matching Haflingers. Music blared from a speaker on the railing as the group cantered down the center of the arena by twos. At the far end, they split apart and circled back to their starting point, keeping close to the railing. He stood quietly and watched them work as they repeated the maneuver. He knew all of the girls except for two. They must belong to another church group.

"What do you think of them?"

He turned to see Connie had come in behind him. She moved up to the rail and leaned on it as he was doing. "The spacing between them needs to be tightened. Other than that, they make a pretty sight."

"Haflingers are so much more than pretty ponies. That's what I want people to see."

"If anyone can prove that point, Fannie can."

"She is throwing her heart into this. I would like to see her succeed for her own sake and not just for the sake of my farm."

The riders came halfway down the railings and turned in to form two circles in the center of the ring, all while maintaining the same speed. One of the horses sped up and bumped into the horse in front of it. Fannie immediately called a halt to the exercise. Noah could hear her talking softly to the inattentive rider. She didn't look or sound upset. It surprised him a little when she patted the girl's arm and said something to make her smile.

The group all walked back to where Connie was standing. There were several unhappy faces on the young riders.

"These things are going to happen," Fannie said. "No one should be upset. Better that they happen in practice and not during a show."

"Have they had a good warm-up?" Noah asked, noting how restless some of the horses were acting.

He couldn't tell if Fannie was happy to see him or not.

"We were late getting started so we went straight into our routine," she said.

"Giving them a warm-up will help both your horses and your riders settle in."

"He's right," Connie said. "Most of the horses have been in their stalls all day and they are eager to stretch their legs."

Fannie got off her mare. "All right, take them around a few times and let them work off some steam."

"Take them outside into the south paddock where there is more room to run," Connie suggested.

"Be back in ten minutes," Fannie said.

The riders happily complied and they were soon out the doors and galloping across the green field, except for one. Susan Yoder had been stopped by George, who was lounging against the side of the barn with a broom in his hand.

"George, I need your help moving a stock tank," Connie called across the way.

"I can help you," Noah offered.

"Thanks, but I'd rather get George away from Susan. She's only fifteen and he's almost twenty. I'll be back when the girls come in." She walked away, leaving Fannie and Noah alone.

"Doesn't Trinket need a warm-up?" Noah stroked the mare's nose.

"We had a good gallop on the way over. What are you doing here?"

"You invited me, remember?"

"Barely, but I didn't expect you to interfere with our practice."

"What did you imagine I would be doing when you invited me? Ah, wait. Let me guess. I'm to sit quietly on the sideline and watch. Is it all right to say I'm sorry for that remark? I had my own mouth-before-brain moment. Does it sound familiar?"

She almost smiled. "Maybe. So, why did you come today?"

"Because it's what I would do if I was your boyfriend. Was your mother upset that I didn't take you home last night, or did you get in undetected?"

"She and *Daed* were still up when I got home.

Mamm was disappointed, but when I told them you had tickets to a Cleveland Indians game, *Daed* said he completely understood. He said he had gone to a game once and has always wanted to go again."

"He should go to the spring training camp. I know several Amish families who time their vacations to do just that. The atmosphere then is not as rowdy as their regular-season games. It's much more suited to a family outing."

"I'll tell him. Did they win?"

"They did. It was an awesome game. It made the long drive there and back worthwhile."

"I'm glad that you got to go, then." She sounded as if she meant it.

"*Danki.* And I haven't thanked you for the brownies and cookies you brought us. Everyone on the team appreciated them, including me."

She peeked at him from beneath lowered lashes. "They didn't choke you?"

He chuckled. "Not a bit. They must have been one of your better efforts."

"They were."

At least she hadn't ordered him off the property. He relaxed and sought to draw her out. "I've seen a few horse drill teams before. Tell me what you are planning for your riders."

"We have covered the basic patterns. Straight line abreast, where horses and riders travel side by side. Then the nose-to-tail exercise, which lines the team up front to back."

"Along the rail?"

"It can be done along the rail, but we are working on a serpentine pattern around the arena. After that move, we line up. Everyone rides single file down the centerline, and when they reach the end of the arena, the first rider and horse turn left. The second rider and horse turn right, and so on. When our two lines meet at the centerline again, riders and their horses pair up and continue riding."

"Sounds complicated."

"It's easier to understand when you see us in action. I'm hoping to add some advanced maneuvers after our first show on Saturday."

"What would that be?"

"A ninety-degree turn. We will ride single file along the rail and then riders turn their horses to the center of the arena at the same time. We go from riding nose to tail to riding abreast. When we reach the other side of the arena, we turn in the opposite direction so we are riding nose to tail again."

"A neat move, if you can pull it off."

"We can. We will."

"I like your confidence. There must be other moves."

"We haven't started practicing them yet,

but once we have the basics down we'll add a mini sweep."

"Explain that."

"We ride along the rail of the arena in an oblique pattern. Someone looking at it from the side would see each horse's nose is in line with the knee of the rider in front of it. What you saw us trying a while ago is called a pinwheel."

"I've seen that done."

"Susan and I hold our horses side by side in the center of the arena, facing opposite directions. We're called the pivots. The other girls line up alongside us, facing the same direction as the pivot rider. Then the whole formation rotates around us while we circle our horses in place."

"So, everyone has to ride a little faster than the rider to her inside in order to keep the line straight."

"That's right. It sounds simple but it's pretty hard."

"I look forward to seeing you pull it off." He liked the eager light in her eyes and the way they sparkled when she was talking about her plans. It used to be that he had to make her mad to enjoy the sparks in those lovely eyes, but watching them shine with eagerness was every bit as satisfying.

Fannie blushed at what she sensed was a compliment from Noah. He seemed genuinely interested in what she was doing. If they could find some common ground it would make it easier to keep up their pretend courtship. "The girls have been practicing very hard. We meet for two hours twice a week. Sylvia Knepp rides for almost an hour to get here."

"That is dedication. I think you mentioned they are all a part of your riding club."

"They are. Before this project we met a few times a month for trail rides and such. Sometimes we would set up jumps for fun. We've shared tips on how to teach our horses tricks." She put her arms around Trinket's neck. "We love horses."

"I can tell."

"Like you love baseball?" He must, if he was willing to date her just to keep playing.

He smiled and shook his head. "I don't think the two compare. Horses can love you back."

It was a good answer, and that smile of his warmed her inside. When he was being nice, she didn't have to pretend to like him.

"Have your parents changed their minds about sending you to Florida?"

"Betsy leaves next Monday unless *Mamm* sees that you and I don't suit."

"Then this fake courtship wasn't such an outlandish idea, after all. If we can keep it up, we'll both have what we want."

The warmth in her chest died away. It was all

make-believe. She was foolish to start liking him and wishing he'd smile at her more often. "I can keep it up if you can."

He looked away. "I reckon I will have to."

The riders returned from their warm-up and lined up beside Fannie. She needed to concentrate on these girls, not her infatuation with Noah. She gestured toward the young riders. "I want you to meet my team."

She started from left to right. "Susan Yoder is riding Carmen. Rose King is riding Goldenrod. Karen Ebersol has Freckles."

"She has white dots on her face and chest," Karen explained, patting the mare's neck.

"Does she have a short temper to match?" Noah cast a sly glance at Fannie.

Fannie ignored him.

"Oh, *nee*," Karen assured him. "She is as sweet as the day is long."

The next girl leaned forward, the only one with dark hair in the group of blue-eyed blondes. "I'm Sylvia Knepp and this is Maybelle. My father works in your family's furniture shop."

"I know him well. He's our master carver. My brother Samuel says he listens to the wood better than anyone he has ever met."

"What does that mean?" the girl beside Sylvia asked.

"This is Pamela Lantz," Fannie told Noah. "She is riding Comet."

He nodded to Pamela. "My brother says a skilled wood-carver must understand what the wood wants to become. He must listen to it. There is no point in trying to carve a ram's head on a piece that is better suited to the grace of a willow tree. The wood won't cooperate. *Gott* places gifts in all people and all things. We must respect that."

"Our gift is understanding horses," the girl on the end said. The last two riders were twins. He couldn't tell them apart, but he made a guess as to who they were.

"My brother Timothy speaks often of Abbie and Laura Lapp, the new girls in his class and how well they do in school, but which of you is Abbie?"

The one on the end held up her hand. "I'm Abbie, and I'm the oldest by ten minutes."

"By six minutes," Laura said with a scowl. "I'm better at math."

Noah noticed Fannie trying not to laugh at their sibling rivalry. "They are riding Copper and Morning Mist."

"Misty for short." Abbie patted her mount's neck.

"All of the horses except Trinket belong to

Connie. She picked the ones with the closest coat colors for the most impressive effect."

"What do you call yourselves?" he asked.

"We didn't want a fancy or prideful name, so we are The Amish Girls," Susan told him with a grin.

He chuckled. "Very appropriate."

Fannie made a little shooing motion with her hands. "We have dawdled enough. Time to work on our pinwheels and on our double circles. Zoe, can you start the music?"

"I'll get it," George called from near the back door. He crossed to the speaker system, fumbled for a minute, and then stepped to the side as a rap song blared forth. The lyrics were disgusting. Sylvia covered her ears. Fannie and the other girls stared at George in shock.

"Turn that off!" Noah yelled.

George started laughing. "It's a harmless little joke. It's funny."

Noah strode to the machine and pulled the plug, silencing the music. "No, it isn't."

George had plugged his phone in to the speakers instead of the MP3 player.

Connie came rushing in. "If you would like to keep this job, George, you'd better start showing more respect to our guests."

"It was a joke, Connie. Don't get bent out of shape."

She unplugged his phone and tossed it to him. "You have work to do."

He slipped his phone in his hip pocket and ambled off.

Connie turned to Noah and Fannie. "I am so sorry. I'll make sure nothing like this happens again."

Fannie wished she could believe that, but George didn't seem to care if their performance benefited Connie. He wasn't putting any effort into saving the stable. He was just out to amuse himself. Maybe he wasn't worried about finding another job, but Fannie knew if Stroud Stables went under, her dream of continuing to work with horses would go under with it.

She couldn't let that happen.

Chapter Six

"We have been invited to visit the Erb family today."

Noah wasn't surprised by his mother's announcement at breakfast on Sunday. It was the off Sunday, a day without church services. Visiting family and friends was a normal way to spend the day, but he knew this wasn't a normal invitation. His mother and Fannie's mother were determined to provide their children with every opportunity to be together. When he and Fannie called off their courtship, he feared both mothers were going to be deeply disappointed.

Noah knew better than to try and get out of going, and he realized he didn't want to miss the outing. He wanted to find out how Fannie's first riding event had turned out. He was even looking forward to telling her about his game.

The morning progressed like any other, but not

as fast as he would have liked. The milking had been done before breakfast by Noah, his father, Mark and Paul. The horses, cattle and pigs were fed after breakfast by Samuel and Joshua. The guinea hens, chickens and ducks were let out of their coops to forage and their eggs were gathered by Noah's mother and Rebecca. Joshua's wife, Mary, and Timothy's wife, Lillian, soon joined the other women in preparing a lunch to take along while Hannah and her dog, Bella, entertained the babies on a quilt on the dining room floor.

Noah checked on Ginger's hoof and washed both the family's buggies before harnessing the horses and hitching them up. It was almost noon before Luke and his wife, Emma, arrived. Once they did, the family made the short drive over to the Erb farm in three buggies.

Fannie's father was standing in front of the house. "Welcome, neighbors. We have set the picnic tables down by the creek. You know the way, Isaac," he said as he waved them through.

"Jump on the back, Ernest, unless your wife wants you to start jogging."

Ernest laughed and patted his ample belly. "She'd better not complain of my size, 'cause it's her good cooking that's done this to me."

Noah opened the door and moved Hannah to his lap to make room for Ernest. It was a tight fit but no one minded. Fannie's father soon had them all laughing at his jovial stories and jokes.

The buggy jolted over the rough pasture track for a quarter of a mile before Isaac pulled to a stop beneath the wide-spreading branches of a group of old river birch trees. A shallow creek flowed across a natural stone shelf formation before tumbling off the edge in a miniature waterfall barely a foot high. There were already two buggies parked in the shade.

Noah set Hannah on the ground and she raced away to join Fannie, Betsy and two other young women who were wading in the water with their dresses hiked above their knees. He could pick out the sound of Fannie's laughter from the others and he smiled. It was good to see her having fun.

He and his brothers carried the ice chests and hampers to the picnic tables set up under the trees. The bishop and his wife were sitting on lawn chairs beside the creek below the falls. They had their fishing poles in the water. Noah's father and Ernest strolled over to join them.

Noah's mother took the hamper from his hand and turned to his cousins. "You boys run along and enjoy yourselves. The two girls with Fannie and Betsy are the bishop's nieces, Margret and Helen Stolfus. I'm sure Fannie will introduce you."

"We met them at the singing last week." Mark

had his gaze fixed in their direction, prompting Noah to wonder which young woman had caught his fancy. Noah and his cousins walked casually to the water's edge.

"Is the water cold?" Noah asked when Fannie caught sight of him.

"*Nee*, it's *wunderbar*." She waded toward him with an ornery grin on her face. She bent low and scooped a handful of water, sending it spraying in an arch toward him. Knowing Fannie, he had quickly moved behind his cousins. Mark and Paul were splattered across their shirtfronts.

Margret and Helen chided her for her mischievous behavior, but Fannie didn't look chastised as she grinned at him.

Noah's cousins took off their shoes and rolled up their pants legs. They were soon exploring the creek with the young women. Paul began his auctioneer call, to the amusement of everyone, as he sold them fish swimming in the stream left and right. Noah sat on the grassy bank and watched. Fannie came over and sat beside him, keeping her bare toes in the water.

"Do either of them catch your fancy?" she asked.

He pretended to look the young women over carefully. "It's hard to tell at first glance. What about you? Mark and Paul are both single, although Mark has a girlfriend back home."

"They seem like nice fellows, but I'm not looking for a man to marry."

"Yet. You aren't looking for a man to marry yet." He'd never noticed what pretty feet she had, small and neat, with dainty toes pink from the cold water. Several tiny fish were investigating them, as well.

"I might wed someday, but I see no point in rushing into something that's lifelong. Do you see the minnows nibbling on my toes? That tickles." She pulled her feet out of the water and tucked them under her hem.

"Fannie, on Sunday night, just before you shut the door in my face, you said something I can't stop thinking about."

"Did I?"

"You said if you had to list my sins, it would take all night. Have I somehow offended you greatly? If I have, I'm truly sorry."

"You were never as bad as some of the boys who teased me. You and I got along so well when we were little, but when we went to school, you stopped being my friend and I didn't have any others."

"Is that why you were always so angry?"

"I come by my bad temper naturally but it has nothing to do with the color of my hair."

"So you say. I'm dying to know how your first drill team competition went yesterday."

She smiled brightly. "Are you?"

"I asked, didn't I?"

She half turned toward him. "You should have seen us. The horses were awesome. Abbie had some trouble keeping Misty in step during the pinwheel, but otherwise the girls did a great job. We took second place."

"Second out of two entries?" he asked to goad her.

"Second out of six entries." She bowed her head slightly, not rising to his baiting.

"Impressive."

"What about you? Did you win your game?"

"It was close, but we pulled it out. Walter hit a homer that brought in the two winning runs."

"I'm glad you won."

"Are you?" He leaned forward to swirl his fingers in the water.

"I said so, didn't I?"

"You also said the water was *wunderbar*." He flicked a few drops at her face.

She giggled and wiped her cheek on her sleeve. "'*Wunderbar* refreshing' is what I meant."

"I thought so." He leaned back on his hands as he grinned at her. Fannie was good company when she wasn't hurling insults at him. How long would it last?

Fannie glanced away from Noah's smiling face. If only he wasn't so good-looking and sweet.

When he smiled at her, she wanted to smile back and bask in his warmth. She kept her eyes focused on the tiny fish darting back and forth in the clear water, in case something of what she was feeling showed in her face. The last thing she needed was to start caring for Noah beyond their friendship.

Wouldn't that be a just reward for concocting their fake courtship? To fall for the fellow who wouldn't be able to get rid of her fast enough come August.

Sitting here enjoying his company wasn't solving anything. She got to her feet. "I should help get the meal on. I see the bishop has reeled in his line. I think that means he's ready to eat."

"Looks to me like he's coming our way." Noah rose to his feet beside Fannie as the bishop approached.

"Good afternoon, Brother Noah, Sister Fannie. The Lord has given us a fine day to enjoy our fellowship."

"Indeed He has," Noah agreed.

"Noah, I would speak with Fannie alone for a few moments, if you don't mind."

Her heart dropped to her knees. Had he somehow learned of their agreement?

"Of course," Noah said, and cleared his throat. He walked away, but glanced back once, his eyes filled with concern.

Fannie gripped her fingers together. "What did you wish to speak to me about, Bishop Beachy?"

"I understand you have formed a riding group with some of the younger girls in our congregation and you are their leader."

"That's true."

"I watched your performance at the fairgrounds yesterday. I wasn't happy to hear the *Englisch* music being played, or to see you girls putting yourselves into the public eye in such a bold way, but as none of you are baptized members of our faith, I won't object to that."

Something in his voice told her he wasn't finished. "But you are objecting to something."

"I'm told you practice at the home of an *Englisch* woman."

At least this wasn't about her courtship. "We do. Connie Stroud is her name. She is allowing the girls to ride her Haflinger horses."

"I have already spoken to your father about this, because I was hoping that he would be able to help, but he says he cannot. Several parents have come to me with concerns."

"What kind of concerns?"

"They feel their daughters are not being adequately supervised. They believe having the girls exposed to *Englisch* ways and music is not good for them."

"What are you saying?"

"Someone other than you must be the group leader. You are young and unmarried. Unless you can find an Amish adult, preferably a married man, to oversee this group, these parents are going to remove their children from it."

She couldn't believe this. "But we have worked so hard."

"Fannie, you can't ask our parents to send their *kinder* to a place that makes them uncomfortable. I won't change my mind about this. It is in the best interest of all our members to know our children are looked after properly."

When he walked away, Fannie sat down on the creek bank and put her head in her hands. Who could she ask? Who would be willing to devote so much time to their project if her own father couldn't?

Noah waited until the bishop was out of earshot before he approached Fannie again. She looked pale and shaken. How much trouble were they in?

He took her hand and pulled her gently in the direction of a thick stand of willows where they would be out of sight. A large fallen log lay in a clump of grass a few feet from the water's edge. Noah led Fannie to it and sat down.

"What did the bishop have to say?"

"That I may have to disband my riding group."

"So this wasn't about us? You and me? That's a relief."

"*Nee*, it isn't about you at all." She jerked her hand from his. "It's about me letting my friends down."

"Don't get angry. Tell me what he said."

"Some of the parents have complained that the girls aren't being properly chaperoned at Connie's place."

"That's ridiculous." The moment he uttered the words he recalled the way George had pressed his attentions on Susan and played such ugly music. He shouldn't have been surprised that there were objections. "What are you going to do?"

"Whatever I have to do. I've come too far to give up now. I can't let Connie down."

"The bishop didn't say you had to stop, only that you and the girls needed a chaperone."

"Preferably a married man."

"Then that's what you will do. I'm sure someone will help."

"Maybe."

"Don't give up before you have tried to find someone. Have faith. If you don't mind me asking, why are you so beholden to Connie? What has she done to earn such loyalty? Besides selling you that pretty mare."

Fannie stared at the creek without answering him. He waited quietly, hoping she would trust him enough to share what was clearly a deeply personal story.

She tossed a piece of bark from the log into the creek and watched it swirl away. "A couple of months after my seventeenth birthday, I went to stay with my cousin over by Walnut Grove. Maddy and I were the same age and as close as sisters. We got along so well because we were so much alike."

"She had the same red hair and hot temper?"

Fannie smiled sadly. "Exactly. We could quarrel one minute like a pair of spitting cats and be laughing and hugging the next."

"She sounds like a *wunderbar goot* friend."

"She was." Fannie closed her eyes.

"Was?" he prompted, guessing the answer.

"She died."

"I'm sorry." The Amish didn't often speak of the dead so he didn't press for more details.

"It was *Gott*'s will. Maddy was determined to try everything during her *rumspringa*." Fannie grew quiet and pensive, staring into the water.

"By *everything*, I take it you mean things you didn't want to try. Drinking? Drugs?" She nodded yes to each.

He stripped the leaves from a willow branch and let them fall into the water. "*Rumspringa* can be a difficult time for some. My brother Luke got into drugs during his running-around time.

It took prison and the mercy of *Gott* to bring him to his senses, but not until my family had suffered greatly. My mother said it was *Gott*'s test of our faith in Him."

"I remember how upset your mother was. I can't count the number of times I saw her crying in my mother's arms."

He looked at Fannie in surprise. "I didn't realize that. She always seemed so strong to me. So unwavering in her faith."

"My father says strength isn't about standing up to adversity with faith as a shield. It's about being brought painfully low but rising again, each and every time, with renewed faith in *Gott*'s plan for our eternal salvation. Our reward is not on this Earth."

"Wise words."

She nodded. "Maddy had a boyfriend. An Amish fellow from a neighboring town who often borrowed a car. At night, Albert would stop at the end of the lane and honk his horn, the signal for us to slip out and go riding around. We went to dances and movies. Sometimes we didn't come home until dawn."

"That's not unusual. I've come in at first light myself, once in a while. You still haven't told me how Connie fits in all this."

"The county fair was on and I wanted to go. Maddy thought it would be a dull time, but she went with me because her boyfriend was busy. Connie was at the fair showing several of her stallions. My father had purchased Trinket for me a few months earlier, so Connie and I already knew each other. She invited us to stop by the horse barn that evening and have supper with her and Zoe in their camper. When we arrived, we could hear loud music from a party going on at the other end of the barn. Connie was busy cooking, but I noticed one of her horses was kicking at his belly."

"Not a good sign for any horse. Colic?"

Fannie nodded. "Maddy wandered down to the party as Connie and I took a closer look at the horse. Maddy came back all excited and said we had to go. Security was making the noisemakers leave. She knew the kids at the party and they were taking a van to another friend's house. I knew Connie would be busy treating her horse, so I started to go with Maddy. Connie stopped me. She said the young men in the group had been drinking heavily all evening and it wasn't safe to go with them. Maddy went anyway."

"You didn't?"

"I almost did, but Connie said her horse needed to be walked and she didn't want to leave Zoe alone in the camper at night, so I stayed. Maddy and her friends were all killed that night when the drunk driver tried to beat a train at the crossing. I would have died, too, if Connie hadn't stopped me."

"*Gott* was great and merciful to place her there, but you chose to stay and help someone in need."

"That's what Connie says."

"I understand now why you feel you must repay her kindness." He hesitated a moment, but decided to share his story, too.

"Walter is the catcher on our team. He dreams of playing major-league ball. And he works toward that goal every chance he gets. The night we were fighting a barn fire over at Silas Mast's place, I got into a tight spot. My coat somehow got hooked and I couldn't get loose. A burning beam was about to come down where I was standing. I couldn't get out of the way. Walter saw what was happening. He pulled his gloves off to free my coat just as the beam fell. He knocked it aside with his bare hands. His dreams of a ball career could have ended then and there. Thankfully, his burns were only minor."

"Is that why you're determined to get your team into the state tournament?"

"It's a big part of my reason. He's an excellent player and he deserves to be seen by the pro scouts that will be at the state invitational. And I like to play ball, too. It will be a win-win if we get there." He decided not to share his own desire to pitch in front of pro ball scouts. For some reason, it didn't seem to be the right time.

"I pray you succeed in helping Walter."

"As I pray you succeed in helping Connie."

"And I'm not sure how I'm going to do that if we have to give up our drill team."

"Surely one of the parents will take over. The girls know how important this is to you."

"This is the busiest time of year for our families. I'm not sure any of them will think they have the time to spare. I am almost ashamed to ask. Connie isn't one of us."

"Can't you practice somewhere besides her farm?"

"If I can't find someone to lead us, I'm not sure what the point will be. I doubt the parents who went to the bishop will allow their girls to travel to other fairs and shows with only Connie and me to chaperone them. I simply have to find someone."

"You will," he said to encourage her. "I have faith in you."

"I hope it isn't misplaced."

"Look on the bright side. The bishop didn't take us to task for faking our courtship."

A fleeting smile brightened her face for a moment. "True, but if he had seen the look of panic in your eyes, the cat would have been out of the bag for sure."

He swiped his hand across his brow. "I felt like a five-year-old getting caught with my hand in the cookie jar."

She laughed out loud. "I imagine you got caught doing something sly almost as much as I did."

"That's the bare truth. Hey, do you remember the time your mother caught us throwing tomatoes against the back of your house?"

"You were throwing them. I was watching."

"You threw some. Fess up."

"Nary a one against the house. I simply fetched them from the garden and handed them to you."

"If I remember correctly, you started throwing them at me. What made you so mad?"

"You said I couldn't hit the house because I threw like a girl. I wanted you to take that back, so I showed you exactly how hard I could throw."

He laughed. "We had some good times in our younger days."

"We did." She smiled and looked down, a pretty blush making pink patches on her cheeks.

When they weren't squabbling, Noah was surprised at how easy it was to talk to Fannie. Her story about her cousin moved him deeply. He understood how strong the bonds of friendship could be, even with an outsider. A week ago he wouldn't have believed it was possible, but he had come to like Fannie a lot. Did she feel the same?

"Sometimes I forget I'm not really courting you."

He held his breath, waiting for her response.

She rose to her feet but she wouldn't look at him. "I always remember it isn't real. Don't worry. Before the end of the summer you will be free again."

He reached for her hand. "Fannie—"

She brushed at the backside of her skirt and started walking. "We should get back to the others. It's getting late. We want our folks to think we slipped away for some time together, but we don't want them to come looking for us."

He had his answer. Fannie wasn't willing to turn their game into the real thing. He should accept that.

But he didn't want to.

Keep walking. Don't look back. Don't ask him if he is being serious. I know he is only kidding. He'll turn it into a joke and I'll start crying.

It was only because her emotions were already raw from recounting a painful time in her life. She wouldn't cry because she liked him far more than she should.

As she came out of the trees, Fannie saw the families were gathered at the tables, waiting for the bishop to lead them in a blessing. A wave of heat crept up her face when she realized everyone was looking her way.

She took a deep breath and kept moving. Were her parents convinced that she and Noah were serious about each other? Convinced enough to take Betsy to the bus station tomorrow? She prayed they were, but realized it might have all been for nothing if she couldn't convince someone to become the team's chaperone.

She took a seat beside her sister at the end of one table. "What's wrong?" Betsy asked.

"Nothing."

"Did you and Noah have your first fight?"

"We've had more than one already."

Betsy folded her hands together. "Don't tell *Mamm* until after I leave tomorrow, please."

"I won't. It's the bishop who has dampened my mood."

"What's he done?"

"He told me I have to give up my drill team if I can't find an adult to chaperone us. Can you think of anyone who might do it?"

"*Daed* might."

"The bishop already asked him and he said no."

"Maybe Timothy Bowman would. There isn't any school over the summer. He likes helping kids."

Fannie looked down the table toward the newlyweds. "*Nee*, for I heard *Mamm* say they'll be leaving on their wedding trip after the school frolic."

"Okay, I'm out of ideas. Maybe it's for the best. It will give you more time to spend with Noah."

That was exactly what she didn't need. It was becoming more difficult to hide how much she liked him. It was easier to pretend she didn't and that she didn't care what he thought of her.

Betsy leaned in close. "Is he a good kisser? I've always suspected he would be."

"That's none of your business."

"Not good, then. Too bad. Maybe he'll get better with practice. Hiram has improved with my coaching."

"Betsy, stop talking and eat your lunch before I pour a glass of this lemonade over your head."

Betsy giggled. "What would your beau think of such poor behavior?"

Fannie glanced down the table and saw Noah watching her. "He'd be glad it wasn't his head."

Chapter Seven

"You haven't said how things are going between you and Fannie. Someone told me the two of you aren't getting along." Noah's mother tried to sound casually interested, but he knew better. She was dying to know every detail of what had taken place while he and Fannie had been out of sight at the picnic the day before. She glanced briefly in his direction and then resumed making sandwiches at the kitchen counter.

"Who said such a thing?" he asked.

"Someone. Is that true?"

"You shouldn't listen to gossip." He took the plate she handed him. It held a thick turkey sandwich and pickle spears. He was on his way to relieve his brother Samuel on the cultivator. The forecast promised rain and they were only half-done weeding the cornfields.

"It wasn't gossip. I'm just curious about the two of you."

"You haven't been curious about the other girls I've dated in the past."

"They haven't been the daughter of my dear friend. I was curious about them, I just didn't show it."

"Fannie and I are getting to know each other. It's too soon to tell if we'll make a *goot* match. She's got a short temper—that's one drawback in her character."

His mother turned back to the counter to prepare sandwiches for the rest of the men who would be in soon. "That's just her young age. Her father has spoiled her and let her run wild too much. She will mature into a fine, demure woman, I'm sure of it."

"Fannie and I are the same age, but you may be right. We're too young to think about settling down. I think I should call it off with her."

"I didn't say that, and it's past time you settled down. Your father and I have agreed you can continue with your ball playing this summer as Fannie and her family don't seem to mind, but your *rumspringa* has gone on long enough."

Of course he couldn't get out of this so easily.

"What makes you believe Fannie will make me a good wife? Because you and her mother are best friends?"

She turned to smile at him. "Because you and Fannie have been friends for ages. Even as babies you played well together."

"I don't remember being friends with her. I remember squabbles and her kicking my shin a time or two."

"You teased each other mercilessly as *kinder*, that's true, but a boy doesn't tease a girl he dislikes."

"And a man doesn't court a girl because he's seeking a friend. He courts her because he's searching for a woman to fall in love with."

"To be in *lieb* is a wonderful, romantic thing, but love changes over time. Friendship, true friendship, endures. I love your father, but he is my best friend first."

She turned back to the stove. "Besides, I see the way you and Fannie watch each other. Your eyes are always seeking her."

He was surprised to realize she was right. He was always looking for Fannie these days. Was she out riding? Was she shopping at his mother's store or working with her father's horses? Was she avoiding him? "She is an unusual person. I'm never sure what she'll do next."

"Her mother tells me she has settled down and is helping with the household chores much more readily that she used to. I would say that is a *goot* sign."

"Don't read too much into that, *Mamm*."

"If you say so. Your brother Luke tells me you have been trying to find a chaperone for Fannie's riding club."

"Without any success. I hope she has found someone. She has her heart set on preforming at the Horse Expo next month to help her friend showcase her Haflinger horses. I never asked, but how do you feel about Fannie's project?"

"The girls are not baptized. It isn't a very modest undertaking, but I have no objection to it. Children should have fun while they can. Adulthood comes all too quickly and childish things must be put aside."

"I'm glad you don't object."

"What does Fannie think of your ball playing?"

"She doesn't understand the game so she doesn't have an opinion one way or the other. She knows it's important to me, just as I know her riding is important to her."

"She will soon find other things that are more important, like having children and making a home for her family."

He tried to picture Fannie in a domestic role, but he couldn't see it. That opinion he kept to himself. His mother wanted to believe they were made for each other and he didn't want to shatter her hopes. At least not yet.

Shame rose in his chest as he realized he would have to one day—but not today.

"Have you heard when Timothy and Lillian are leaving on their wedding trip?" he asked, to change the subject.

"They have decided to postpone it until the spring."

"Any reason?"

"Timothy says they want to spend more time with her family and he knows your father could use his help in the furniture shop this summer, since you haven't been available."

He pushed back his chair and swallowed the last bite of his sandwich. "Which is another way of telling me I'm slacking on my work. I'll do better. I don't have to see Fannie as much as I have been."

"That was not my meaning and you know it."

He laughed and kissed her cheek. "If Fannie were more like you, I'd marry her in a heartbeat."

She gently pushed him away. "Get out of here and stop trying to flatter me. If she is the one *Gott* has chosen for you, I pity her."

On the following Thursday, Noah drove his buggy to Connie's farm hoping that Fannie had been able to find someone to supervise her group. She was alone in the riding arena, taking a Haflinger gelding over a set of low jumps set up along the perimeter. When she cleared the last jump, she turned toward Noah and rode over.

He reached over the railing to pat the horse's neck. "I don't see the others, so I take it you haven't had any success in finding a chaperone."

"I haven't. Everyone I have talked to is either busy or they don't approve of what we are doing. What harm is there in demonstrating our riding skills?" She sounded so dejected. It wasn't like Fannie to admit defeat.

"I imagine some people see it as prideful."

"It isn't about us. It's about the horses."

"It's about Connie's horses and she is an outsider. Distrust of outsiders runs deep for many Amish. I'm sure some people believe she is exploiting their children for her own gain."

She scowled at him. "Whose side are you on?"

"I'm on your side, but I can see both sides. I would do it if the bishop agreed."

Her face brightened. "You would?"

"Unfortunately, he said it wouldn't be proper, as I'm a single fellow."

"I'm grateful that you asked. What's the use? I might as well see if Connie can get some of her money back for the entry fees she had to pay. I feel like such a failure."

"You can't take the whole blame upon yourself. Perhaps this is *Gott*'s will for Connie."

"I know, but it makes me angry."

"Does being angry at *Gott* help?"

She had the grace to look ashamed. "*Nee*, it does not."

"Then don't let bitterness into your heart. It's hard to weed out when it takes hold."

"I was so sure I could do this."

"Did you get your sister off to Florida?"

"We did, and I miss her already. Which is funny because we were always fighting."

"It was the same with me when my brothers moved out. Now that I don't have to share a room with anyone, it's lonely at times. Timothy and I became a lot closer when it was just the two of us."

"Where are he and Lillian going for their wedding trip?"

"They were going to stay with her folks in Wisconsin, but they have decided to postpone the trip until the spring."

He suddenly straightened. "Have you asked Timothy and Lillian if they would chaperone your group?"

"*Nee*, I didn't think they would be here."

"They're the perfect couple to do this. They're married and respected teachers. No one could object to their supervision."

"Let's go ask them."

"Now?"

"Have you got something better to do?"

"I don't, but aren't you supposed to be exercising Connie's horses?"

"I have one more to ride after I'm done with Benny, but why don't I saddle the other one for you and we'll exercise them by riding to Timothy's place. Connie won't mind if we can secure a chaperone."

Noah had ridden astride many times as a boy, but it had been a while. "I wish Timothy hadn't given up his cell phone. It would have been so much easier to call him. Which horse is it?"

"Joker. He's in stall number six. Do you think Timothy might agree? I'm afraid to hope."

"Never be afraid to hope. First Corinthians, chapter thirteen—'and now abideth faith, hope, charity, these three...'"

"'But the greatest of these is charity,'" she finished, and he smiled.

Fannie found herself smiling back at Noah. He was willing to help her and her team. He genuinely seemed to care about her efforts to help Connie. If he had been trying to endear himself to her, he couldn't have gone about it in a better way. It felt wonderful to have his support.

Ten minutes later, they were cantering along the edge of the river toward the covered bridge at Bowmans Crossing. Timothy and Lillian lived on the other side of the ridge, beyond the river.

Both horses were eager to run, but Noah held his mount beside Fannie's mare.

They passed by his house before they reached the bridge. His mother was in her garden. She raised a hand and called a cheerful greeting. Fannie waved back.

"It makes me feel rotten," Noah said under his breath.

"What does?"

"*Mamm* is so happy we are dating. I'm sure going to hate to tell her we've broken up when the time comes."

"I know what you mean. My mother is happy about us, too."

Fannie slowed her mount to a walk as they entered the covered bridge, alert for oncoming traffic. Cars sometimes sped through without slowing. Once they were on the other side, Fannie urged her horse to a faster pace, eager to find out if Timothy would become their manager. The road curved around the hillside where the school was located and then zigzagged back and forth up a steep ridge through the dense woods.

At the top of the ridge, Fannie pulled her horse to a stop. "Let's rest them a minute. I love this spot."

A natural clearing off to one side of the road presented a breathtaking view through a break in the trees. The farmland spread out below was a colorful patchwork of fields and woodlands laid out like a giant crazy quilt. The clearing also provided a secluded spot for young couples, Amish and English, looking to be alone.

She glanced at Noah. Had he come here with any of the girls he'd dated before? She couldn't bring herself to ask.

He swung out of the saddle, and walked back and forth. "My legs aren't used to straddling a horse. I should have driven my buggy and tied these horses on behind. It would have been the same amount of exercise for them."

"Take a hot bath tonight, that will help any sore muscles. Connie likes her mature horses to be ridden three or four times a week. It helps them behave well for her riding classes. If someone comes looking to buy a horse, she can let them ride with confidence, knowing the horse won't buck or balk."

"Makes sense, but that's a lot of horseback riding each week. How many does she have?"

"Forty, but only twenty-five of them are for sale."

"Forty? That's a lot of hay and oats as well as saddle blisters. I can see why she needs to broaden her market."

"The breed is gaining in popularity. We just need to show more people what they can do."

"I admit I've always thought of them as little draft horses."

"That's what they were bred for in Europe. They came from the mountainous areas of Austria and northern Italy. A stallion known as 249 Folie was born in 1874. He is considered the foundation sire. Modern Haflingers can trace their lineage back to Folie through one of seven bloodlines."

"You really are taken with the breed, aren't you?"

"Because they try hard to do whatever we ask of them."

He mounted Joker again. "Let's hope Timothy can save The Amish Girls team." He groaned as he swung up into the saddle. "I haven't ridden astride in ages. I'm rusty."

"You ride well."

"The horse has a smooth gait."

"It's a breed characteristic. They are gentle and willing to please. They make wonderful pets for children."

"Will your father be raising them instead of Standardbreds anytime soon?" he asked with a grin.

She laughed. "I doubt it. He loves a high stepper as much as you do."

"I like it when you laugh."

She blushed. "It's not like it's a rare thing."

"Rare enough. You worry too much."

"I know that to worry is to doubt *Gott*'s mercy and love, but I can't help it. Don't you worry that you will lose a game or not be invited to the state tournament?"

"I play my best, and if it is *Gott*'s will that we lose, I accept that."

"When I lose I think it's because I didn't try hard enough."

"You'll be more content if you learn to let go of your fear of failure."

"I'm not afraid of failing."

"Aren't you?"

Maybe she was afraid of failing, but she was more afraid of disappointing her friend. She glanced at him from the corner of her eye. "Why did you come with me today?"

"Why did you ask me?"

"Timothy is your brother."

"Lillian is your friend. You didn't need me to come along. Maybe you like my company," he suggested.

"You can be fun sometimes. When you are being nice."

"A compliment from *karotte oben*. Things really have changed."

"I'm perfectly willing to scold you if you feel you need it."

"*Nee*, I prefer you this way."

"What way is that?"

"Not throwing things at me or kicking my shins."

She tipped her head. "Some of those were accidents, some you deserved. What are you going to do when baseball season is over?" she asked to change the subject.

"I'm not sure." He grew somber. "A lot depends on if we make it into the tournament."

"How so?"

He hesitated for a long moment. "My coach, the guys on my team, they tell me I'm really good. Good enough to play professional ball."

She couldn't have been more surprised if he'd said he wanted to fly airplanes. "Are you considering that? I confess I never imagined you living a worldly life. You seem so happy among us."

"*Gott* has given me a mighty gift. If I'm to use it to honor Him, I don't see how I can accomplish that here."

"'Neither do men light a candle and put it under a bushel, but on a candlestick, and it giveth light unto all that are in the house.' Matthew 5:15." She understood his dilemma.

"Exactly. I'm not like Luke was when he left. He hated all things Amish, hated the restrictions and rules. I see their purpose. I love my family and they would be disappointed if I left, but perhaps that is *Gott*'s plan for me. I will know by the end of the tournament."

"How?"

"If I get an offer from a professional scout, then I will know my place is elsewhere."

"Does your family know this?"

"I'm not ready to tell them."

"No wonder you agreed to my proposal. I had no idea how important playing ball is to you."

He chuckled. "Who would have thought that you and your Haflingers would ride to my rescue? The Lord moves in mysterious ways. Let's go see if Timothy can ride to the rescue of The Amish Girls."

They headed down the winding road on the far side of the ridge. Fannie had plenty of time to think about the confidence Noah had shared with her.

It had never entered her mind that he would leave the community. The thought of just how much she would miss him was sobering. And all the more reason to keep a tight rein on her feelings for him.

It didn't take them long to reach Timothy's home. They found the newlyweds together in the garden.

"Noah, this is a surprise." Timothy stopped working and leaned on his hoe.

"A pleasant one," Lillian said, rising to her feet

with her apron full of new potatoes. "Come inside. I have a fresh pot of coffee on the stove."

"Have you bought yourself a new pony?" Timothy asked, taking the reins as Noah stepped down.

"Just exercising this one for a friend. You own a Haflinger, don't you, Lillian?" Noah asked.

"I do. Goldie is a wonderful cart horse. What can we do for the two of you?"

Fannie followed Lillian into the house. "I have something to ask you and your husband."

"Let's sit. I'll get the coffee." Lillian dumped her load of potatoes in the sink and washed her hands before getting out mugs.

When everyone had a cup, Fannie glanced from Lillian to Timothy. "My riding club has been preparing a drill team program at Connie Stroud's horse farm."

"Noah has told us the bishop won't let you continue there," Lillian said.

"Not unless we can find someone to chaperone us. I was wondering if you might take on the task, Timothy?"

"Me? I don't know anything about equine drill teams."

Noah leaned forward. "You don't have to. Fannie can manage the team. What she needs is someone respectable to make sure the girls are not unduly influenced by their *Englisch* surroundings."

"Have there been undue influences?" Timothy asked.

"No," Fannie said quickly.

"Yes," Noah said a second later.

Fannie took a deep breath and nodded. "Some of the girls were made uncomfortable by the attention of Connie's hired man and his music."

"Then the bishop was wise in his decision," Lillian said softly.

"Connie has said it won't happen again," Fannie stressed.

"She may mean well, but few *Englisch* understand our ways well enough to judge what is acceptable and what isn't." Timothy took a sip of his coffee.

"How much time would this involve?" Lillian asked.

"Four hours a week and travel to several local shows before we go to the Horse Expo next month."

Timothy scratched the new beard darkening his cheeks. "That's a big commitment, Fannie."

"I know it is." She folded her hands on the table and waited. If God wanted her plan to continue, He would move Timothy to accept. Noah had told her to have faith and she was trying.

"I'll help all I can," Noah said. "I can take care of chores here for you, if need be."

Lillian took a sip of her coffee and put her cup

down. "I would be interested in watching the girls from our school perform."

Timothy nodded slowly. "I reckon it might be considered an educational opportunity for them. Horses supply our transportation and help us till our fields. Everyone should have an understanding of how to train and handle them."

"The girls learn cooperation, not just between horse and rider, but between each other. It takes practice and commitment. To do it well takes a team effort." Noah glanced at Fannie, and she smiled her thanks.

"Kind of like baseball," Timothy said.

"Kind of," Fannie agreed.

"If it is educational and does not conflict with our teachings, I believe it to be a worthwhile project." Timothy sat back and winked at his wife.

"Then you'll do it?" Fannie pressed her palms together.

"*Ja*, we will do it." He reached for his wife's hand across the table.

"In fact, we were hoping to be asked," Lillian said with a smile. "I belonged to a riding club when I was a girl. I made some lifelong friends and wonderful memories."

"I must speak to the bishop first, but I'm sure he won't object. When do we start?" Timothy looked to Fannie.

"Tuesday at six o'clock in Connie Stroud's riding arena."

Timothy nodded. "We will see you there."

Noah stood and held out his hand. "*Danki, bruder.* You have made a whole gaggle of girls happy."

"*Ja, danki*, Timothy. This is *wunderbar.* I can't wait to tell everyone." Fannie jumped to her feet, too, almost knocking over her mug in her haste. Lillian caught it before the contents spilled into Noah's lap.

Feeling foolish, but still excited, Fannie left the house. Outside, she spun in a circle and threw her arms around Noah. "I'm so happy!"

He slipped his arms around her waist. "I'm happy that you're happy."

"Are you?" She stared into his eyes, amazed at the way they darkened.

"I said so, didn't I?" Slowly, he bent his head toward her, and she knew he was going to kiss her.

Chapter Eight

Noah waited, expecting Fannie to turn away from him, but she didn't. He should stop, but he wanted to taste her sweet lips, feel them pressed against his. The strength of those desires shook him to his core. Unsure of her reaction, he lifted her chin with his hand. "I would like to kiss you, Fannie."

"Then why are you talking?" She closed her eyes.

Because he was a fool and because he didn't want to take advantage of her innocence. She was excited that her drill team could continue. He was only her pretend beau. She deserved a real one. Someone who was sure of his place in her life. God had not yet shown Noah if he belonged in the Amish world or the outside world. Until that changed, he didn't have the right to kiss her. "I don't think this is the time or place."

She stepped back, a hurt expression filling her eyes. "Let me know when you think the right time might be and I'll see if I'm busy or not."

Sweeping around him, she headed to her horse.

"Fannie, let me explain."

She didn't slow down. Mounting her horse, she slipped Joker's reins loose and took off at a gallop with both horses, leaving Noah behind.

He heard the door of Timothy's house open and his brother came out. "I couldn't help noticing Fannie looked out of sorts just now. Is something amiss between you?"

"She drives me *narrisch*." This whole masquerade was insane. It was tying him up in knots. Did she like him or not? One minute he was sure she did. The next minute she was furious with him and he didn't understand why.

"My wife can drive me crazy, too. *Gott* designed women that way. It keeps us men humble."

"The moment something isn't going right, Fannie's temper takes over and she flies off the handle instead of listening to reason."

"Noah, I've seen you gentle a skittish filly that no one could handle. It took time and effort, but you never gave up. Now Ginger is the sweetest horse on the farm and the one *Daed* trusts to take *Mamm* where she needs to go. You must put some of that effort into understanding Fannie."

"Horses are different than people."

"Are they? Don't we respond to patience and kindness? Don't we want someone to understand our fears, to reward us when we have done well? The biggest mistake you can make in a relationship is to guess at what the other person is feeling. You have to ask and you have to listen. Honesty is the only way two people can live their lives together in harmony."

Honesty was something sorely lacking in his relationship with Fannie. "I'll have a talk with her when she cools down."

"*Goot.* Can I give you a lift home?"

"Can you take me to the Stroud farm? Willy is there."

"Sure. If we hurry, maybe we can reach the farm before Fannie leaves."

"No need to rush. I think it's going to be a while before her temper cools."

"What did you say to her?"

"The same thing I always seem to say to her. The wrong thing."

"I thought Noah's team has a home game at the fire station today. Aren't you going to go watch him?" Fannie's mother asked on Saturday afternoon, as she washed a strainer full of fresh beets from the garden.

Not if I can avoid it.

"I want to finish my chores. Are there more

clothespins? I need some to hang out this last load of laundry." Fannie put the heavy hamper full of damp dresses and pants on the kitchen table.

"There are some in a package on the shelf above the washer."

"I just missed seeing them. *Danki*."

"I can hang those out. Go watch Noah's game. I'm sure his whole family will be there. All the men say he's a *wunderbar* pitcher, as good as the *Englisch* professional players."

"I've heard that." She wasn't in any hurry to face Noah. First he'd said he wanted to kiss her, and then he said it wasn't the right time. Her eagerness for his kiss had to be what changed his mind. He'd been repulsed by her lack of modesty.

She had certainly made a fool of herself. Standing with her eyes closed waiting for his kiss like a dope. He must have been laughing at her the whole time. In spite of telling herself not to fall for him, she had anyway.

"I'm sure Noah is modest about his talent, as any *goot* Amish man should be."

Noah had his finer points. Fannie had to admit that. "When he pitched a no-hitter, he said it was because his team did a great job fielding the ball and kept the other team from getting on base."

"I'm glad to hear that. Go to his game. I can hang out the laundry when I'm done with this."

"He'll play for nine innings, there's no rush.

I'll hang these and wash the kitchen floor and then I'll go. I promised you I'd be more help around the house and I meant it."

"I admit I'm surprised at how much help you have been, child. Your father says you aren't neglecting your barn chores, either."

Fannie picked up the hamper. "Taking care of the horses isn't a chore in my book, but I don't think I realized how hard you and Betsy work."

Glancing over her shoulder, her mother smiled. "Taking care of my home and my family is not a chore in my eyes. It's a privilege to serve the Lord thus, for these are His greatest gifts to me."

"I never looked at it that way." Fannie always hated being inside when a beautiful day outdoors begged her to take one of the horses for a gallop across the fields. She assumed her mother had given up such pleasures for the drudgery of being a wife because it was expected. Was she truly happy in her role?

The front door opened and Fannie's father rushed in. "Fannie, Willow has gone into labor. I knew you'd want to be with her until she gives birth."

Fannie's pulse surged. She had been with Willow's mother when she was born and had helped raise the beautiful Standardbred mare. This was Willow's first foal, and Fannie was hoping for a filly that would stay on the farm and become a broodmare instead of being sold.

As quickly as Fannie's elation rose, it settled again. She had too much to do to spend the day in the barn. "Let me know what she has, *Daed*."

A small frown creased his brow. "All right. I will come get you when her time is close."

"She is going to watch Noah play ball," her mother explained.

His frown vanished. "*Ach*, I reckon I knew the day would come when horses would take a back-seat to a boyfriend. Came sooner than I was expecting."

"Not for me, it didn't," her mother said, scrubbing away at the beets.

"It's as it should be, I reckon," he said with a wink for Fannie. "But I will miss our times together working the horses."

"I'll still be here. Noah and I don't seem to be getting along that well."

"Oh?" Her mother turned around. "Is this why you are dragging your feet to watch him play?"

"Had a quarrel, did you?" Her father's sympathy was almost more than she could bear.

"Something like that."

"Don't be afraid to admit when you are wrong," her mother said.

Tears pricked the back of Fannie's eyes. "Why do you assume I'm the one in the wrong?"

Her mother came and put an arm around her. "Because I know what a temper you have. If the two of you won't suit, so be it. But don't throw away a chance at happiness when two simple words are all that is needed. Saying *I'm sorry* heals many hurts. If you wait because you think the other person must say it first, the wound grows out of proportion to the injury. Forgiveness heals the forgiver as well as the forgiven. Do you want to tell us what happened?"

Fannie shook her head. How could she admit she was upset because Noah hadn't kissed her? He had offered to explain, but she had been too humiliated to listen to him.

"Seek him out and tell him what is troubling you. You won't feel better until you do."

Maybe her mother was right. Fannie nodded. "I'll speak to Noah after his game tonight."

Fannie hefted the laundry basket and went outside. Having made the decision to listen to Noah's explanation didn't make her any more eager to face him.

Noah considered the sign for a low inside pitch Walter was giving him. He nodded. It was a good call for the left-handed batter. Winding up, he checked the runner on first and threw with all his might. The batter swung, but the ball smacked into Walter's glove untouched for a third strike.

The runner on first made a dash for second base, but Walter fired a beeline throw to their shortstop, Simon. He tagged the runner out ending the fourth inning. The hometown crowd cheered loudly.

Noah jogged off the mound and checked the lawn chairs and quilts along the baselines on his way to the dugout. There was no sign of Fannie among the Amish men and women enjoying the game. He tried not to let his disappointment show. Clearly, she was still angry with him.

"Noah, you're up," Eric said, nodding toward the batter's box.

After selecting his favorite bat from the group hanging on the fence, Noah took several practice swings and stepped up to the plate. A second later, pagers began going off around the field. Noah, along with the other firefighters present, tossed their equipment to anyone close and ran toward the fire station building, where the large double doors were going up as the siren overhead began to sound. Noah didn't give the game another thought.

"We have a structure fire reported at 2391 Raintree Road," Eric explained, as the men began pulling their fire gear over their ball uniforms.

Noah knew the address. It was an Amish home about five miles away. He prayed the family was safe.

"At least I don't have to go pick anyone up,"

Walter said, pulling on his coat. "Our crew is already here."

John Miller, Joshua and Timothy rushed in. As married men, they no longer played for the team, but they always came to home games to cheer on their fellow firefighters.

As soon as everyone was geared up they climbed into the smaller truck with Walter behind the wheel. They pulled out behind the main engine and followed it out to the highway. When they turned the corner, Noah caught a glimpse of Fannie standing beside her cart in the parking lot. She raised a hand and waved.

He waved, too, and sat back with a sense of profound relief. She had come to see him play, after all. He couldn't believe how happy that made him. When he could, he would find a chance to explain himself. If she would listen.

Fannie yawned. It was well after midnight as she sat on a bale of hay in the barn watching Willow's new colt struggle to his feet. She jumped and pressed a hand to her heart when Noah sat down beside her. "You startled me."

"Sorry. I was trying not to disturb them." He nodded to the new mother and baby.

"How did you know I was out here?"

"I saw the light on, but thought it must be your father out here. So I threw some pebbles against your window. I picked the wrong one. Your father opened it and told me where you were."

"You really threw pebbles against my window? Why?"

"That's how a fellow gets a girl to sneak out late with him, isn't it?"

It was true. Most Amish couples courted in secret after the parents had gone to bed, but she wished he had come over because he wanted to see her, not because it would make their false courtship more believable. "My folks will not doubt we are serious now."

"I thought as much, after your *daed* opened the window. Fannie, I came to apologize to you."

"That's not necessary. I'm the one who stormed off in a fit of temper."

"I think I gave you just cause. Can we talk about it?"

She stared at her feet. "Is there anything to say? I thought you were going to kiss me and you didn't. My lack of modesty repulsed you."

He lifted her chin with one finger, making her look at him. "Is that what you think? Nothing could be farther from the truth. I wanted to kiss you, Fannie."

"So, why didn't you?"

He clasped his hands together in his lap. "It didn't seem right. We are only pretending to court. The man who kisses you should be a man who genuinely deserves that honor."

"You kissed me once before."

"I was young and impatient then. I wasn't thinking about the right thing to do."

"Did you…did you like kissing me?" She couldn't believe she'd found the courage to ask him that.

"Very much. I like you Fannie. I do. You drive me nuts, but I like you. If you want to call this courtship off, I understand. You don't have to worry about going to Florida and you have your chaperone now."

"If we break up, won't your parents expect you to end your *rumspringa*?"

"I can deal with that, if they do."

"This was my idea. I will hold up my end of the bargain."

"Are you sure?"

"I am. And I'm sorry I rode off and left you yesterday. That was childish of me."

"Actually, as stiff as I am from my one-way ride, I'm not sure I would have been able to walk if I had ridden back with you. Can we start over and be friends, Fannie?" He covered her hand with his.

The warmth of his touch spread through her body. "We can't start over," she said, "but we can be friends from now on out."

"*Goot.* I'd like that. Have you named this young fellow?" He nodded toward the foal.

He still held her hand. She didn't pull away. His touch was comforting. "Not yet. I'm waiting to see what kind of personality he has, first."

"I'd call him Wobbles. Look at those long legs. He has no idea how to make them work."

She grinned. "*Wobbles* wouldn't be a very good name if you were trying to sell him as a buggy horse."

"You're right. *Fancy Stepper* would be a better name." He let go of her and rubbed his hand over his face.

She gazed at him in the lantern light. "You look tired. Was it a bad fire?"

He nodded. "It was a shed, not the house, thank the Lord, but it took us a long time to put it out. The farmer had his winter store of firewood in it, and it was really close to his barn. It took all we had to keep it from spreading."

"That's a shame. I hope no one was hurt."

"One of the neighbors that arrived before we did suffered some smoke inhalation and minor burns trying to toss out as much wood as he could. He and the farmer saved maybe a quarter of it."

"What was the cause? Was it arson?" Her community had been devastated by a series of arson fires the previous fall. If not for the generosity of outsiders and English friends like Connie, many of those affected would have been ruined, as none of the Amish carried insurance. Having it was seen as doubting God's protection and mercy.

"It wasn't arson. One of the sons went to fetch his mother more wood for the cookstove. He accidentally knocked over his kerosene lamp."

She glanced at the lantern glowing above their heads. "That's why *Daed* only allows battery-operated lamps out here."

"Same with my folks. I'm sure the family's church will bring them enough wood to get through the winter and more. I know I'll be taking some over."

"That is one of the best things about being Amish—knowing no matter what tragedy befalls us, the community will rally around us and lighten our burden."

"That's true of the Amish, but also true of many *Englisch* folks. Besides our fire crews, all of the opposing team members followed us to the scene to help fight the fire tonight. They aren't even from around here."

"My dad says people are born good. Any evil that grows in them is because they weren't shown the ways of goodness as they grew up."

He nodded. "That's why being a parent is such a great responsibility."

She glanced at him out of the corner of her eye. "Do you hope to be a parent someday?"

"Sure. I see how it has changed my brothers. I see how happy and content they are. Maybe *fulfilled* is the word I'm looking for."

"You don't think they resent giving up their freedoms, even a little?"

He shook his head. "If they do, I've never seen a sign of it."

She kept her eyes on the young colt nosing his mother for a meal. Somehow it was easier to talk to Noah in the quiet stable with the darkness held at bay by a single lantern. "Do you think your sisters-in-law are content, too?"

"I've never given it much thought. I don't see why not. *Gott* has given them what most women seek. A man who loves them. Children to be loved in turn and a home where they can be happy together as a family. Wouldn't you be content with that?"

Would she? "I'm not sure."

"Why do you say that?"

"My *aenti*, my mother's youngest sister, is only five years older than I am. We were close until she fell head over heels in love and married at eighteen. They moved away to Illinois to live with his family. We still exchange letters all the time."

Fannie looked at Noah. "She isn't happy in her

marriage. The husband she loved so much isn't kind or comforting. After three miscarriages, she fears they will never have children, and he blames her for that."

"I'm sorry for your aunt. Her life must be difficult. She is fortunate to have you to console her. Fannie, we can't know the reason *Gott* chooses some of us to suffer in this world. He has a plan far beyond our simple understanding."

"I know that, but it worries me to see how easily love can blind us and lead us to mistakes. Connie loved the man she married, but he left her for another woman."

"For every sad story of broken love, you can find dozens, hundreds of people who have endured and grown old together with unwavering love for one another. My grandparents, my parents, your parents. I imagine even your grandparents in Florida will tell you they still care for each other. Am I right?"

"*Ja. Grossmammi* says *Grossdaadi* has the same twinkle in his eyes as she saw the day they met."

He tipped his head as he gazed at her. "I didn't know I should be watching for twinkling eyes. I'll keep that in mind from now on."

She felt the heat rush to her cheeks at his scrutiny. "Will you be at the school frolic on Friday?"

"Sure. Will you?"

She shrugged. "I'm thinking about it."

"*Goot*. I hope you come. It will do you good to get down from your horse and mingle with people for a change."

"I mingle."

"But you'd rather be riding."

"And you'd rather be playing ball."

"Ah, that's where I have the advantage. Someone will suggest we get up a ball game after the work is done at the school."

She chuckled. "Someone like you."

"Only if no one else suggests it first. I should be getting home. I just wanted to thank you for coming to my game tonight and explain about the other thing."

"I'm sorry I jumped to the wrong conclusion, and I'm sorry I didn't get there sooner to watch you pitch tonight."

"There will be other chances to see my fastball in action."

"I'm glad you stopped by." She was, and she didn't try to hide the fact. There was an ache in her heart because he wanted to be her friend and not something more, but she would learn to live with that.

He smiled. "I'm glad I did, too. It was nice to meet Fancy Stepper over there."

The colt was getting accustomed to his feet.

Feeling frisky, he tried a little jump that turned into a scramble to keep upright.

Noah and Fannie laughed at his antics. "Corker. I'm going to call him Corker," she said.

"That's a fine name for a horse with an attitude like his. *Ja*, it's a *goot* name. Would you like to ride home from church with me tomorrow, Fannie?"

A swirl of happiness made her almost giddy, but she kept a calm face. "I'd like that very much."

"*Goot*. So would I. *Guten nacht*, Fannie."

"Good night, Noah."

As he walked out into the dark, Fannie pulled her knees up and wrapped her arms around them. Noah hadn't been repulsed by her behavior, as she had wrongly imagined. He had been thinking of her feelings, not of himself. By jumping to the wrong conclusion, she had done him a disservice and spent an entire day feeling miserable.

Now that she knew they could be friends, a load had been lifted from her shoulders. She didn't have to worry about what to expect from him. His friendship was a fine gift and one she would cherish.

She didn't pause to wonder why the prospect of seeing her friend again tomorrow filled her with such eagerness.

Chapter Nine

Fannie rose early the next morning with a sense of excitement bubbling inside her. She was going to see Noah again soon. Recalling their evening in the barn left her feeling happy and hopeful. He was willing to be her friend, a dear friend.

As she entered the kitchen, the pale pink light of dawn provided a colorful view through the kitchen window over the sink. The few wispy clouds she saw promised a fine day.

She put the coffee on and grabbed the wire egg basket from the wall on the front porch. Keeping busy was a way to make the morning go faster. The dew was heavy on the grass as she hurried barefoot across the front yard.

Her parents kept a dozen laying hens. Their small henhouse was a movable pen and coop combined, painted white with a green roof to match the other buildings on the farm. It held two hinged nesting boxes with removable back panels that allowed for easy cleaning and access to the eggs. Happily, there were ten eggs, and all the chickens were accounted for. The rooster crowed his impatience to be let out. She opened the pen door and the flock raced out to roam the farmyard during the day and eat their fill of crickets and grasshoppers.

Fannie noticed the glow of a lamp down at the barn and guessed her father was already feeding the horses and making sure Willow and her colt were okay before they left for the church service. It was being held at the home of Luke Bowman. The family lived less than two miles away, so her family wouldn't have to make an early start.

Wiping her wet feet on the welcome mat, Fannie opened the door and saw her mother was up and getting breakfast ready.

"Did you see your father?" she asked, glancing over her shoulder at Fannie.

"*Nee*, but I saw a light in the barn."

"Tell him to hurry. We don't want to arrive late."

Fannie smiled. It was the same thing her mother said every Sunday there was a service. To Fannie's recollection, they had never been late, but still her mother insisted that they might be if her husband didn't hurry up.

Fannie's mother cut several slices of the ham

that she had cooked the night before and transferred them into a skillet before packing the rest of it in a hamper. A light noon meal always followed the service. Each family brought enough food to share.

"I'll see if I can help him with the chores." Fannie put the eggs on the counter and started back outside, but stopped when she saw her father was already hitching a horse to the family buggy.

"Looks like he's finished. What do you need me to do?"

"Cut some lettuce from the garden and bring me in a half-dozen nice tomatoes."

Fannie pulled a kitchen knife from the drawer and went out to fetch the produce. Searching among the tomato plants for ripe fruit, Fannie smiled as she remembered the time Noah had shown her how he threw a baseball using a few tomatoes that made a satisfying splat when they hit the strike zone he had marked on the side of the house. They had been spotted by his mother, who had scolded them both for being wasteful.

"You seem happy this morning," her mother said, looking over the garden fence.

Fannie placed several ripe tomatoes in her bowl. "I was thinking back to some of my childhood scrapes."

What if her friendship with Noah grew into something more serious? Was she prepared for that? The idea of being courted in earnest didn't repulse her the way it once had.

"Remind me to share some of mine with you one of these days."

"*Mamm*, I can't imagine you getting into trouble, even as a child."

"Ha! With four sisters in our house we were always getting up to something."

"Like what?"

"Like tying someone's braids around the bedpost while they were sleeping."

Fannie gaped at her. "You didn't. Whose?"

"Mildred was the eldest and was always hogging the bathroom getting ready for school in the mornings. We thought we could have our turns before we untied her."

Fannie chuckled. "Did it work?"

"*Nee*, she hollered so loud that our *daed* rushed in to see who was being murdered. Needless to say, we never pulled that trick again."

"Did Mildred get the point?"

"She took even longer after that. Look at me, wasting time talking. I came out to ask you to bring in some green onions, too."

Fannie handed her the bowl of lettuce and tomatoes over the fence. "I'll be right in with them."

Her mother started to turn away, but paused. "You seem more content today, Fannie. Did you patch things up with Noah?"

"We did." She smiled to herself.

"I'm so glad. Whatever the cause, I like this change in you. I'm so glad you and Noah have found each other. I may be getting ahead of myself, but I do love fall weddings."

"I'll get those onions for you." Fannie's excitement drained away.

It was one thing to imagine her friendship with Noah could blossom into a stronger relationship, but the reality was that when the summer was over, her pretend courtship with him would end, too.

Then she would have to pretend it didn't matter if he moved away to the English world—or if he remained Amish and chose to court another.

She pulled herself up short. That kind of thinking was selfish. She would be happy for Noah no matter where his life took him. A husband, even someone as progressive as Noah, would never accept her working for Connie.

Fannie and her parents arrived at Luke and Emma's place well before eight o'clock. Buggies and horses were already lined up along the corral fence. The bench wagon was being unloaded in front of the hardware store that Luke ran with his wife and his wife's two younger brothers.

The house was attached to the store by a covered walkway. Inside the building, the shelves of merchandise had been built with large casters that allowed them to be rolled back against the outer walls, making an open space where the benches were being set out.

Fannie followed her mother around to the entrance to the house and into the kitchen where the women were making preparations for the meal after the service. Dishes were being brought out; glasses were cleaned and stacked in rows. Coffee cups and mugs were arranged on the end of the kitchen counter. No meal after an Amish service was complete without plenty of piping hot black *kaffee*.

Emma took the hamper Fannie had carried in. "It's good to see you, Fannie. So, tell me, how is it going with you and Noah?"

"Fine," Fannie answered, feeling like a fraud each time she was asked about him.

"Just fine?"

"For now."

Emma bit the corner of her lip. "Lillian said the two of you had a quarrel. Give him a chance. The Bowman brothers are fine men. I almost didn't give Luke a second chance, but I thank *Gott* every day that I did. I couldn't be happier now."

"Noah and I worked out our differences," Fannie said to reassure her.

Relief filled Emma's eyes. "I'm happy to hear that."

"So am I," Rebecca said from behind Fannie.

Apparently there was nothing secret about their courtship, except that it wasn't a real one.

The service lasted almost three and a half hours. Bishop Beachy was in fine form and gave a stirring sermon about forgiveness and the need to guard against pride. He and his ministers took turns preaching without notes. They spoke as God moved them.

Afterward, as the families filed out of the building, Fannie looked around for Noah. She had seen him when she came in, but he was gone from his place at the back when the service ended. She finally caught sight of him standing by his father's buggy, speaking with Rob and Simon Beachy. From their animated gestures, she guessed they were talking baseball.

Noah noticed her and nodded in acknowledgment. A grin lifted one side of his mouth and brought a light to his beautiful forget-me-not blue eyes. She smiled in return and went to join her mother and several other young women who were setting out lawn chairs in the shade of a large oak tree.

Her mother leaned close. "Will you be staying late with the other young people this evening?"

"I will be staying, but I'm not sure I'll be staying late."

"Someone is taking you home?"

"*Ja, Mamm.* Someone is taking me home."

Susan Yoder approached her. "We're getting up a volleyball game. Would you like to join us?"

"Sounds like fun, and I have some news to share with you." Fannie jumped up to follow Susan to where a dozen girls and young women were choosing sides as two young men strung the net for them.

Fannie gestured for the girls from her team to gather around. "Timothy Bowman and his wife are going to manage our team. We can start practicing again on Tuesday."

The girls clapped with delight. "Have you told Abbie and Laura?" Susan asked.

"I plan to ride over to their home tomorrow. We've missed an entire week of practice. That means we'll have to work doubly hard to make up for lost time."

"We could stay for an extra half hour each time we meet," Susan suggested.

"Only if you girls are willing to do that," Fannie said.

"I am," Pamela said, looking at her teammates.

They all agreed. Fannie couldn't have been more pleased with their dedication. The Amish Girls would ride again, and together they would showcase the wonderful horses of Stroud Stables.

After the game and the meal were over, a few of the families began leaving. Most would stay until late in the evening, visiting with one another. Fannie was taking the hamper and empty dishes back to her father's buggy when Noah caught up with her.

"Let me carry that for you." He reached for the hamper.

He took hold of it but she didn't let go. "I'm capable of carrying it."

"I know you are. I didn't offer because I thought you were infirm. I offered because I want to assist you and because my brothers are watching."

She glanced behind them. All four of his brothers were lined up along the porch staring in their direction.

He took the hamper from her. "They want to make sure you aren't still mad at me."

"Emma and Rebecca quizzed me this morning about our quarrel."

"What did you tell them?"

"That we had worked out our differences."

"*Goot* answer." He opened the buggy door and put the hamper on the backseat.

Fannie looked toward the porch and saw his brothers had been joined by their wives. Noah's parents and Fannie's parents were seated in the shade with glasses of lemonade in their hands, but they were staring in Fannie's direction, too. Everyone wanted to see how they were getting on. If this kept up, she would have to hang a sign around her neck announcing No Quarrel Today.

She sighed heavily. "I'm beginning to feel like a prize mare at the auction. Everyone in your family is looking me over. Next, they'll want to check my teeth. Luke and Emma will probably report back everything we do or say at the singing tonight."

He chuckled. "I have a solution, if you don't mind missing the party."

What was he up to? "I don't if you don't."

"Then just keep walking. Our getaway buggy is near the end of the row."

"You mean leave without telling anyone?"

"I do."

"What a great idea."

He reached for her hand. "You aren't the only one who has them."

She giggled and twined her fingers with his, feeling like a schoolgirl again, slipping away to play hooky.

They reached Noah's buggy and he helped her in. It took only a minute for him to back out of his parking space and set Willy in motion.

"Where to?" he asked when they reached the end of the lane.

"I don't care. Just somewhere where no one will ask how things are between us. I'm afraid I'm going to blurt out it was all a joke."

"I know the feeling. Want to go up to the overlook again?"

Fannie shook her head knowing it would get busy later. "Let's go to my family's picnic spot. No one will go there this evening."

"The Erb picnic spot it is. Do you mind if I pick up my fishing pole?"

"Not so long as I don't have to clean any fish."

"I will clean my own catch."

"And mine?"

He gave her a lopsided grin. "If you catch any. Fishing takes patience."

"And you think I lack patience?" She tried to hold back a grin and failed.

"Think? I know you do."

"Ha! We shall see about that."

After stopping at home to grab his fishing pole, Noah drove his buggy over to Fannie's place. She dashed inside to change out of her Sunday dress and grabbed a quilt for them to sit on. Noah drove them down to the creek on Fannie's property feeling more lighthearted than he had in ages. While he unhitched Willy and left him to graze, Fannie spread out the quilt beneath a tree.

He settled on the blanket beside her and leaned back against the trunk of the tree. It was a beautiful sunny day with high, white cotton-ball clouds drifting across a blue sky so bright it made his eyes water to stare at it.

But it wasn't the sky that drew his attention. It was the sparkle in Fannie's eyes when she laughed at something he said or when she pointed out the antics of a squirrel in the tree overhead.

She pulled her knees up and wrapped her arms around them. "I do wonder what they are saying about us now."

"The squirrels?"

"*Nee*, our families."

"I'm sure everyone has an idea about where we went and what we are up to."

"Will Luke and Emma be upset that we didn't stay for the singing?"

"Luke understands. It wasn't that long ago that he was courting Emma."

She nodded toward his pole. "Aren't you going to fish?"

"Later. At the moment, I feel lazy and the grass under this blanket makes it wonderfully soft. This was a *goot* choice."

"*Danki*. This is one of my most favorite places in the whole world."

"It's a pretty place, all right." The trees were large with wide-spreading branches that let only dappled sunlight through. The murmur of the creek as it slipped over its rocky course provided a soothing sound, as did the birds and insects in the trees.

"I used to come here a lot. I would bring a book and spend all afternoon reading when I was about twelve," Fannie said.

"Reading was Timothy's thing, not mine."

"What was your thing? Baseball?"

"Not at that age. I was a birder."

She looked at him in surprise. "A what?"

"A birder is a serious bird watcher," he said in a solemn voice.

"You're teasing me."

"Nope. I kept a log of all the species I identified. I still have it somewhere. Did you know there are more than one hundred types of common birds that call Ohio home?"

"I did not know that."

"I had a great-uncle who lived near the Killbuck Marsh. I used to go and stay with him for a few weeks each year. He got me started birding. He knew everything about birds. We would hike out into the marsh at dawn and spend the whole day trying to find as many species as we could. Each Christmas, he would send me a card with a beautifully drawn picture of one of the rare birds he'd seen that year. When he passed away, I sort of lost interest in it. Then I discovered baseball, and that became my passion."

"Oh, how I wish I had known that. To think of the names I could have called you. Birdbrain, featherhead, dodo bird. My cup would have runneth over with joy."

"I see where this is going. Revenge for carrot-top."

"Pure and simple."

"Really? The name *Noah* didn't supply you with enough fodder for taunting?"

"It was a biblical name. It didn't feel right to make fun of you for that. Having the name *Fannie*, on the other hand, did bring out the worst in some of the boys."

"I never teased you about your name."

"Just about my looks. I don't see how that is any better."

He folded his arms and looked her up and down. "They have improved considerably over time."

"Coming from a birdbrain, that's quite a compliment."

"I knew I never should have shared that story. Do you still come out here to read?"

"I haven't in years. Riding and training horses takes up all my time now."

"Things change for all of us, I reckon."

"That is true. What will you do if you can't play professional ball?"

"Stay on the farm and work with my *daed* and brothers."

"As the youngest son, the land will come to you when your *daed* is gone."

"I hope I can be as good a steward to the land as he has been. What are your plans after the Horse Expo?"

"I'll keep working for Connie. If things go well for her, she'll employ me full-time."

"You truly love working with horses, don't you?"

"Do you think it's strange that I want to devote my life to it?"

"It's unusual, but then you've always been an unusual person. I mean that in a good way, before you get upset and resort to name-calling again. What will you do if Connie can't save her stable?"

"I don't know. It's something I can't consider."

"Isn't working with your father satisfying? You could always continue training his horses."

"I love my father and I enjoy helping him, but I want to train saddle horses, not just buggy horses, and I want to give riding lessons."

"Couldn't you do that at home?"

"My parents would object to having *Englisch*

people coming in and out. You know how it is. I would have to conform to their Amish standards."

"My family does a lot of business with the *Englisch*."

"My parents are more old-fashioned in their beliefs than yours. They are already pressuring me to join the church. If and when I do, I will have to give up riding."

"Are you considering not joining?" He should have seen that coming, but he hadn't.

"Maybe. I don't know. I'm not ready to make that decision."

They were both on the fence about the most important decision young Amish adults had to make.

"Is there anything I can do to help?" he asked, genuinely wishing he could do something for her. He wanted to see her smile again.

Her eyes grew sad. "When you are a famous ballplayer and traveling to faraway cities, send me postcards so I can keep track of you."

"Sure," he answered quickly.

The only trouble was, he didn't want to go far away from Fannie. He'd never had someone he could share everything with, the way he could with her. Their make-believe courtship had sparked a true and deep friendship, for him, at least. He wasn't sure how she felt, but he hoped she felt the same.

Perhaps it was a foundation they could build into a real courtship one day.

If God wanted him to stay.

Chapter Ten

"You look like you have something serious on your mind, Fannie."

Sometimes Connie was too observant. Fannie had been thinking about Noah and her growing feelings for him, ever since their outing two days ago, but she wasn't sure she was ready to share them. "I was mentally preparing to start work with our new boarder. I have time before the group arrives for practice."

They were seated in Connie's office, a converted bedroom in her house, trying to make her income from riding classes cover the coming month's feed bill. It wasn't stretching. The expense of transporting eight horses and eight Amish girls to various fairs in the region had put a dent in their emergency funds. The rest was earmarked for the Expo.

Connie tipped her head to the side. "Is that

all? Are you sure it isn't Noah that has you looking glum?"

Maybe it would ease her mind to share her feelings. "You guessed it."

"Want to talk about it?"

"Noah and I have gotten to be good friends. I've never said that about anyone but you. I think Noah understands me."

"Is that a bad thing?"

Fannie shrugged. "Of course not, but how do I keep from liking him too much?"

"Are you saying you're in love with Noah?"

"Maybe. *Nee.* I enjoy being around him. He's great company when we aren't fighting."

"By *fighting* I hope you don't mean he's abusive."

"Of course not. He's kind and he's funny. He teases me and makes me giggle."

Connie leaned back in her chair and twirled her pencil between her fingers. "Giggle. So you are half in love with him."

"Am I?" Was she?

"I'd say so."

"What do I do about it?"

"Fannie, if you can't commit to the relationship, you need to end it."

That wasn't what she wanted to hear. "Why should I give up being friends with him? He's a wonderful man."

"Because staying friends with him will be incredibly difficult. A woman's heart is made for love. I'm not saying a friendship between a man and a woman is impossible. I'm saying it's often the stepping-stone to love. How does Noah feel about you? Do you know? Has he told you?"

"He teases me like I'm his kid sister. I'm not sure how he feels, but it doesn't matter. We don't want the same things out of life. I won't let us become more than friends, but I won't give that up."

"More power to you if you can make that happen. The heart has a way of overlooking even the most difficult problems and tumbling you into love before you know it."

This wasn't getting her anywhere. "I should get to work. Are you going to come watch me?"

"Oh, like I would miss it. Let's go."

Fannie walked into Connie's arena ten minutes later with their new boarder on a lead rope. The black-and-white gelding kept his head high and flinched with every move she made toward him. Using the end of the rope, she swung it past him. He jerked away violently. She raised her hand quickly and got the same response. Anger made her press her lips together. The poor fellow had known unkindness, if not outright abuse, from someone.

Breathing deeply, she let go of her anger and

concentrated on sending calm signals to the horse. She unsnapped the lead and let him loose. He took off at a run.

Noah entered the riding arena and saw Fannie with a tall paint gelding. The horse wore a halter, but Fannie didn't have him on a line. She was simply standing in the center of the arena as he galloped around it. She held a coiled lead rope in one hand. Noah leaned on the rail to watch her. What was she up to?

Fannie caught sight of him and grinned, but she kept her attention on the animal traveling around her.

Connie came over and stood beside Noah. "Fannie is very taken with you."

"I am taken with her myself."

"I can tell that you love her."

He drew back in surprise. He wasn't in love with Fannie. He cared for her. Deeply. But that wasn't love. Why did this woman think he was?

"We aren't that serious, but we have become very good friends." That much was the truth.

"I'm relieved to be wrong," Connie said.

"Why is that?"

"Because I believe Fannie will never be happy in a traditional Amish marriage. She's a woman who needs her freedom. She loves horses and she has a tremendous gift with them. She's what we call a horse whisperer."

"And what is that, exactly?"

"Someone who can communicate with horses on a level that few of us even understand. Plus, she is the best riding instructor I have ever met. Look at all she has done with her girls in such a short amount of time."

"You praise her highly."

"She has earned it."

"She thinks a lot of you, too."

He had never looked at Fannie's affection for horses as a gift. He had trained a number of them. He understood that it took patience and repetition to bring out the best in an animal. Connie clearly saw something more in what Fannie did.

Connie nodded toward the paint horse nervously pacing around the enclosure. "This is a horse I'm boarding. The owners brought him in yesterday. They recently purchased him for their daughter, but they say he's a problem for them to handle. He's head shy and difficult to catch."

"They chose poorly for their daughter."

"Not everyone who buys a horse is an expert. The previous owner should have alerted them to the issue. I suspect he wasn't an honest fellow. They thought the horse was simply spirited."

"Then they should get their money back."

"After Fannie explained to them why the horse

was acting up, they decided that returning him to his former owner was not an option for them."

"I see. So they asked you to retrain the horse?"

"Fannie offered as soon as she saw what was wrong. See how the horse keeps moving? Their natural instinct is to fight or to flee. Their first choice is always flight."

"What is she doing now? Why is she just standing there?"

"Fannie is becoming the herd leader. She is going to show by her body language that she is a safe place."

When the horse came by she raised her arms and the horse moved away.

Perplexed, Noah said, "I thought she wanted him to come to her?"

"She hasn't invited him to join her herd."

Fannie continued to drive the horse forward until he had made a dozen laps around the arena. Twice, she closed the distance between them and forced the horse to switch directions. It went on for fifteen minutes.

Connie leaned closer to Noah after the horse had made several more circles of the arena. "Watch the horse's ears. See how he is keeping his inside ear toward Fannie. She is holding his attention while his other ear is listening to the rest of the building. When he starts slowing and moving his mouth, he's relaxing."

Fannie lowered her arms but kept moving more slowly. As she did, the horse began to close the distance between them as he circled her. When he was walking calmly, she turned her back to him and he approached within a few feet.

She took several steps away and the horse followed her. She turned left and he continued to follow close behind her. When she stopped to face him, he stretched his nose toward her and she rewarded him with a rub on the forehead.

"This is called joining. He has confidence now that she doesn't mean him harm. She's a safe place to be, and he'll remember that. He'll never forget the abuse someone gave him, but he can get past it now. Not all humans are bad."

"I thought I knew horses pretty well, but I see I have more to learn."

"If I can get this stable back in the black, Fannie is the one who can help me keep it that way. She has a job here for as long as she wants it. If she marries, she will have to give this up, won't she?"

"If Fannie joins the church, she will take a vow to follow the rules of our congregation, the Ordnung. Working outside the home is rarely permitted for a woman unless she is helping with her family's or her husband's business when she marries. Once the children come, she must give her family her full attention."

Connie gestured toward the middle of the arena. The horse that had been so fearful was resting his head on Fannie's shoulder. "Do you think she can give that up? I couldn't if I had her gift."

Fannie started jogging and the horse followed her. She darted one way and then another as he followed her every move in a game of tag. Laughing, she stopped and put her arms around his neck. The horse didn't flinch.

Noah realized he'd never seen Fannie so carefree. The half-formed idea that had been growing in his mind withered and died. If he didn't get picked up by a scout, he had been considering courting Fannie in earnest. She had an amazing way of getting inside his defenses. Just as she had done with the horse she was training.

Watching her doing what she loved, he knew he couldn't ask her to give it up. The most he could hope for was to continue their friendship. It was far better to accept that now. Before he made the mistake of falling in love with her. As she walked toward him, he was determined not to let his disappointment show.

Pasting a cheerful smile on his face, he opened the gate so she could come out and closed it before the horse came, too. The animal stood at the gate waiting for her to come back in.

Noah turned to Fannie. "Where did you learn to do that?"

"Do you remember me telling you about the fair I went to years ago?"

"Of course. The night your cousin died and *Gott* prompted Connie to step in and save you."

"While Maddy and I were exploring the fairgrounds that afternoon, I saw a man give a demonstration on this technique. He was amazing. They brought in three horses he'd never seen before, all with different problems, and he gentled each one of them. One in less than fifteen minutes. I knew I had to learn to do it. Then, well, you know my cousin was killed and I came home. I tried to show my father how it was done, but he said the old ways were best. He's not cruel to his horses, but he believes he has to show them he is in charge."

"That must have been frustrating for you."

"It was. Then I took this job working for Connie. After that, I was able to use what I knew and expand my education. Connie was as excited by the technique as I was. She purchased videos I could watch on her computer. We have even traveled to several events where—I don't call it horse training, I call it people reeducation—it was taking place. I learned something new every time."

"Will your friend react the same to me as he did to you?"

"He will if you are interesting enough."

Noah pretended indignation. "What's that mean? You don't think I'm an interesting fellow? What kind of thing is that to say to your beau?"

He opened the gate and stepped in with the horse, watching for any signs of agitation. He saw none. Instead of reaching for the horse, Noah walked a little way into the arena. The horse followed him after a brief hesitation.

Turning, Noah faced the animal, which still wasn't displaying any signs of agitation. He had his ears forward, his head was slightly lowered and his posture was relaxed. Noah held out his hand. The horse came forward to sniff him. After rubbing the animal's forehead, Noah took hold of his halter and led him back to Fannie. "He doesn't seem head shy to me."

"He was, wasn't he, Connie?" Fannie grinned at her friend.

"He jerked George off his feet when George took hold of his lead rope."

Connie came through the gate and clipped a lead to the horse's halter. The animal submitted meekly. "With a little extra people training for his owners, he should make a good family horse."

She led the paint away, leaving Noah and Fannie alone. Noah slipped his hands into the front pockets of his jeans. He was still in awe of what he'd seen. Fannie's famous temper was totally absent. "Timothy should be here soon. He wanted to be here before the girls began to arrive."

"I'm so thankful he has agreed to be our chaperone."

"He prefers the term *manager*."

"Manager it is."

"I have to say I'm really impressed with your gift, Fannie. I had no idea."

"Does it rank up there with your fastball?"

"Hmm, let me think. Nope."

"Oh! You are conceited, Noah Bowman."

"Ah, now you are the one looking for a compliment. Not very plain behavior, if you ask me."

"I didn't ask you. Don't you have somewhere else to be?"

"Are you two quarreling again?" The question came from Timothy, who was watching them both with mirth brimming in his eyes.

Noah winked at Fannie. "Not at all, *bruder*. Teasing is how we show our affection for each other, isn't it, dear?"

"Sure. And pigs have learned how to fly," she snapped back.

Noah chuckled. "I believe Hiram mentioned that."

Fannie closed her eyes and shook her head. "I have to go get Trinket. My team is arriving. Timothy, I can't tell you how much I appreciate what you are doing."

"It's all in the name of education. Mine, most of all."

Noah noticed George come in the far door, but at the sight of both brothers, he turned and walked out. Hopefully he understood the message. He wasn't to bother the girls again.

It didn't take long for the excited group of girls to offer Timothy their collective thanks and ready their mounts. When they were lined up by twos, Fannie called for the music to start and they rode out.

"I don't know much about this sport. I see the concept, but what are the challenges?" Timothy asked Connie, who had come back in to stand beside them.

"*Stay in line* is the first rule of a drill team. No matter what, the riders need to keep their positioning even and stay straight. It doesn't matter if the horse is trotting, pacing or cantering, the audience will only notice the spacing and unity of the group. The riders have to be ready to shift up or down to maintain the line. Riders on the inside of a turn have a smaller radius and need to hold back, while the horse and rider on the outside of the turn has to hustle. Notice how Abbie is lagging behind the group during turns."

"Abbie, keep up," Fannie called out.

"I'm trying."

"She's going to have to push her horse harder to make up that extra step," Connie said.

"Maybe not. Fannie, hold up a moment." Noah moved out into the ring. He drew a line in the dirt with his boot and walked off a dozen paces before drawing a second line.

Fannie rode over with a scowl on her face. "What are you doing?"

"Measuring strides. Pamela, Abbie, I want you to trot your horses across the first line all the way to the second one at the same speed."

After the girls did as he asked, Timothy joined Noah to examine the hoofprints. Fannie swung out of the saddle. "I don't see what you're trying to prove. Abbie needs to push her mount harder to keep up."

Noah shook his head. "Misty needs to be the second horse on the inside of the pinwheel."

"We have the girls arranged according to their height. Having Pamela on the inside won't work."

"Then they need to trade horses. Is there a reason they can't?" He looked at the girls. They looked at each other and shook their heads.

"I'm not sure trading horses in the middle of the season is a good idea. Connie and I paired these girls with these horses for a reason. They have grown used to each other."

"Come look," he said. "Count the number of strides Misty took compared to Comet. See?

Misty's stride is a good four inches shorter than Comet's. If we switch their places in the pattern, Abbie won't have to try so hard to keep up with the group."

"I see what you are saying." She didn't sound happy about it.

"If it doesn't work, it doesn't, and you go back to what you were doing."

She sighed heavily. "We can give it a try. Switch horses, girls. Zoe, start the music again. From the beginning, ladies."

The group went through the entire program without pausing. Abbie was able to keep pace in the pinwheel and she was grinning from ear to ear when they finished. She patted her new mount's neck. "That was easier."

Noah walked up to Fannie's side and cupped his hand to his ear. "What was that, Fannie? Did you say *you were right, Noah*?"

She tried to hide a smile. "It pains me, but you were correct this time."

"Don't mention it."

"Any other suggestions?"

He tapped his lips with one finger. "Not at the moment, but I'm sure something will occur to me."

"Don't you have ball practice or something else you need to do?"

"Nope."

"Are you on call? Isn't there a fire some-where?" She was struggling not to laugh.

"Nope."

"Can you just go away and leave us in peace?"

"You want me to go?"

"*Ja*, Noah."

"See how much better your communication skills have become, Fannie?"

"Are you going or not? Because I have work to do."

"Okay. I leave you and your group in Timothy's capable hands. Only there is one more thing."

Fannie rolled her eyes. "Tell me now before I die of curiosity."

"You want to showcase the horses' skills, don't you?"

"That is our entire plan in a nutshell."

"I saw you take some pretty impressive jumps on Trinket and on the gelding you were riding the other day. Why not add some jumps to your rou-tine? Haflingers make fine show jumpers. You said so yourself."

Fannie opened her mouth and closed it again.

Noah turned to his brother. "I love it when I can leave her speechless."

Fannie was torn between feeling foolish that she hadn't thought of it and wanting to hug Noah for the suggestion. "You are right."

Noah cupped his hand to his ear. "What was that, Fannie? Did you just say I was right again? Twice in one day!"

"Yes, birdbrain, I said you were right again. Even a blind pig finds an acorn once in a while. However, I must admit it is an excellent idea," she added before he took exception to her quaint saying. He gave her a wounded look but kept quiet. She turned to Connie. "What do you think?"

"If we set them up in the center, you can use it as part of your entry. Say, four jumps of slightly increasing height?"

"We'll have to leave enough room for our pinwheel in the middle."

"Then that won't work."

"Set them around the perimeter, far enough away from your pattern area that they won't interfere," Noah suggested. "I assume the arena at the Horse Expo is larger than this one?"

Connie nodded. "Much larger. We don't want to detract from the flow of the ride. You girls can swing wide at some point and go over them. Perhaps at the end of the program."

"Will we be allowed to add jumps?" Susan asked. "Don't we have to follow the rules of the competition?"

"That's the beauty of it," Connie said. "We won't be competing in the drill team event at the Horse Expo. I've pulled in all the favors I could manage and even pressured some members of the Haflinger Association who were friends of my father to give us the breed spotlight. Our mission is to show the crowd and the country what awesome horses Haflingers are."

"What do you mean when you say 'show the country'?" Fannie asked.

Connie grinned. "The Expo is a televised event. You knew that, didn't you?"

No one spoke. She looked around the group and her smile faded. "Will that be a problem?"

Chapter Eleven

"It's going to be televised? Are you sure?" Lillian asked, looking from her husband to Fannie.

Seated with Noah and Timothy in Lillian's kitchen, Fannie blew out a deep breath. "That is what Connie told us. Do you think it will make a difference to the bishop? You don't think he'll put a stop to us again, do you?"

Timothy shook his head. "I'm not sure how he will feel about it, but we have to let him know."

"Sometimes it is better to ask forgiveness than permission," Noah said.

Timothy frowned at him. "This is not one of those times, little *bruder*."

"I thought I would offer it as a suggestion." Noah folded his arms over his chest.

"It isn't a bad one." Fannie could see the merit in it.

"They may be right," Lillian said, drumming her fingers on the tabletop.

"How so?" Timothy asked.

"Nothing has changed. The bishop has said these girls are not baptized and the rules of our church do not yet apply to them. People were taking pictures of you at the fair when the bishop was watching, weren't they, Fannie?"

"A lot of them were, but most people took pictures from a distance or from the side, so our faces weren't in them."

Lillian laced her fingers together and leaned forward. "Then Connie will have to insist that the television people do the same. No close-ups of the girls' faces. No mention of names. She must ask them to respect our religious beliefs. If they agree, I say there is no need to worry the bishop over this one small detail."

"And if they don't agree?" Timothy asked.

"Then we place the decision in Bishop Beachy's hands." Lillian sat back with a smile.

Timothy stared at Lillian in amazement. "I had no idea my wife was so devious."

Her mouth dropped open. "Husband, how can you say that?"

"I say it with great unease."

Lillian chuckled and leaned forward to pat his hand. "Have no fear. I will never deceive you, my love."

"You say that now, but what if *Gott* ordains that I am chosen to be a minister and then a bishop someday? Will you seek to keep other small details from my view?"

She shrugged. "I shall cross that bridge when I come to it."

Timothy looked to Noah. "Be cautious when you choose to wed, Noah. It can't be undone."

Lillian giggled. "As if you would undo our vows. I know you better than that. Fannie, are you coming to the frolic on Friday?"

"I am. My parents, too."

"It will be wonderful to finally have enough room for all our students," Timothy said.

Noah stood. "I hope we have plenty of willing hands to share the work."

Timothy rose, too. "I don't think we need to worry about that. All the children are excited about helping."

Lillian pulled a piece of paper from her pocket. "I had a note from my friend Debra Merrick. She is planning on coming. She's eager to begin teaching health and well-baby classes in the new wing and wants to do her part in getting it ready."

Debra was the local public health nurse. With Lillian's help, she had become well-known and well liked in the community after she and her brother helped raise money for the families affected by the arson fires. She held a well-baby clinic once a month and taught classes on food safety and other topics afterward. She took great pains to be respectful of their Amish beliefs. Fannie had met her several times and liked her.

"Are you ready to go, Fannie?" Noah settled his ball cap on his head.

"I am." She had ridden with him to Timothy's home to discuss what they should do about the Horse Expo being televised. She had been too upset to enjoy the buggy ride out, but she was looking forward to being alone with him on the ride home.

Outside, he helped her into the two-wheeled cart he had chosen to drive that day. It was the same type of cart she and her mother drove for short trips around the community when the weather was nice.

As they started up the hill, he glanced her way. "Feeling better about this now?"

"I am. If Connie can get the Expo to agree to our requests, I don't see a problem."

"Have faith that it will work out."

"I hope so. I truly do. We are so close to pulling it all together." She was almost afraid to believe it would happen.

"I was thinking."

"Not again, Noah. You know that strains your birdbrain." She tried not to giggle, but she couldn't help herself.

"Ha-ha! Why did I ever tell you that story?"

"Just to make me happy. What were you thinking?"

"Forget it."

"I want to know."

"I was thinking that your Haflingers have one more skill we could add to the program."

She tipped her head. "What skill would that be?"

"What are we doing right now?"

"They are wonderful horses, Noah, but they can't carry on a conversation."

"Be serious. What am I doing?"

"Annoying me?"

"Fannie! I'm trying to help. I'm driving a horse in harness."

Her mind began whirling with the possibilities. "A second act."

"Exactly."

"A driven drill team consisting of Haflingers."

"The same horses, driven by the same riders."

"Versatility is the mark of a horse trained at Stroud Stables."

"There you go. It doesn't have to be an elaborate program. Basically repeat the patterns you've already taught the girls, only in carts instead of on horseback. Are all the horses broke to harness?"

"They are. Connie insists on it because her

Amish customers want horses to pull their buggies and carts. They aren't looking for riding stock, while her *Englisch* customers most often want ponies for their children to ride. The girls have been driving carts since they were five or six. They shouldn't have any problem."

"And you had the nerve to call me a birdbrain."

Fannie linked her arm through his. "I'm sorry. This is a fine idea. I can't wait to tell Connie and see what she says about it."

"I have my cell phone. Do you want to call her?"

Fannie was tempted but she shook her head. "*Nee*, it can wait. Good news is best shared in person."

"Spoken like a true Amish woman."

"Danki." Fannie kept her arm linked through his all the way to Connie's farm.

Two days later, Fannie and her group practiced unsaddling their mounts and getting them into harnesses as quickly as possible. With two girls working together on each horse and the adults helping the youngest members, they soon had the time cut down to an acceptable amount.

Connie raised her hands. "The crowd will simply have to listen to music for a few minutes."

"Or you can be giving a short lecture on the

breed history and characteristics," Fannie said. She knew people would find it interesting.

"Not me." Connie shook her head. "I can't speak in front of people. I get horrible stage fright, but I will give something to the announcer to read."

"You can stand on the back of a galloping horse in front of hundreds of people, but you can't speak in public?"

Connie gave her a sour look. "Everyone has some kind of phobia."

"Have you heard from the Expo people about our television restrictions?"

"I haven't, but I should hear something soon. I know some folks think I'm exploiting these young women to improve my financial standing, but I draw the line at asking them to go against their fundamental religious teachings on national television."

Fannie looked at her riders. "Are we ready to try this?"

They all agreed. The Amish Girls went through their main routine with ease while Timothy, Noah and Connie looked on. After the last pattern was complete, they swung out to take their mounts over the hurdles set up along the walls and then went out the open barn doors. Outside, the girls unsaddled their mounts and then harnessed them. It was time-consuming and before all eight horses were hitched to their prospective carts the girls were sweating and flustered. Once they entered the ring again, they were able to settle down and drive with precision.

Connie applauded loudly when they were done. "You make it look so easy."

Fannie stood in her cart. "Practice the same time next Tuesday. Remember, we are giving a show on Wednesday at the Mount Hope Horse Auction. Everyone should be here by nine o'clock. Connie will have a van to take us and a hauler to take our carts, so please drive your carts that morning. She will be taking the horses in her horse trailer. If the show goes well, we can skip practice on Thursday and plan on having one on Saturday at noon. I'm very proud of all you girls have accomplished. I couldn't be riding with a better group if I tried."

After the practice was over, Noah drove Willy home while Fannie rode beside his buggy.

"What did you think of it?" she asked.

"It was a little ragged at the end, but it's nothing that can't be smoothed over with a little more practice. I think the crowd at the Expo will be mightily impressed with the breed and with Connie's ability to train them."

"That's all I can ask," Fannie said with a satisfied smile.

When they reached her lane, she pulled to a

stop beside him. "You're still planning on coming to the frolic, aren't you?"

"Of course. Will I see you there?"

She smiled and nodded. "I'll be there."

He touched the brim of his hat. "Until then."

Fannie trotted Trinket toward home, eager for tomorrow to arrive.

Noah was helping his brothers unload the lumber they would need at the school and keeping one eye out for Fannie and her family. Where were they?

"What's wrong with you?" Samuel asked.

"Nothing, why?"

"Then watch what you're doing. Two-by-fours go over there." He gestured toward a stack of lumber beside the school building.

"Right." Noah picked up the boards he'd added to the pile of siding and carried them to their proper place.

Two women came out of the school building. One was his sister-in-law Lillian. The other was an English woman, the county health nurse, Debra Merrick. A young woman in her midtwenties, Debra was dressed in a simple black skirt and a white blouse. Her low-heeled black shoes were sensible and sturdy. Debra's blond hair was cut short with curls clustered around her face. She was a pretty woman, but he liked Fannie's wild red curls better.

"Why do you call it a frolic?" Debra asked.

"The name just means a social and work event that takes place in our Amish communities," Lillian explained. "It can be anything from a quilting bee to a barn raising. Whatever needs doing, we ask for volunteers and they show up. Today, the men and boys get together to do a few hours work in putting up the new school wing, and we feed them. That's a frolic."

"Your good food is one wonderful thing I've discovered about Amish country. I've had to go up a dress size already, and I've been here less than a year."

Debra stared at the slab of concrete waiting to be covered. "Can you really get a building up today?"

"Noah, what do you think?" Lillian asked.

"The frame will be up by noon and the rest will be done by five if we get enough help."

"I'm willing to do my part. Where are the tools? I've always wanted to use a saw." Debra looked around.

Lillian steered her away from the lumber. "Let's make sure we have enough to feed everyone, and then we can help the men later."

The frolic was set to start at eight o'clock. Men trickled in until there was a crew of about fifteen.

Fannie and her family finally arrived and Noah felt a surge of happiness at the sight of her. She wore a dark blue dress with a white apron, and for once she didn't have jeans and boots underneath. There was nothing to mark her as different from the other women gathered to work. All of them went inside the school building.

Some of the younger boys were playing with tools and trying not to cause mischief. Timothy took charge of them and put them to work. Paul came up to Noah carrying a case hung over his shoulder by a thick strap.

"What have you there?" Noah asked.

Paul opened the case and pulled out a microphone. "It just came today. It's my sound system. It operates on batteries as well as electricity. With this I can run an auction anywhere."

He switched it on. "Brothers and sisters, welcome to the Rider Hill School frolic." His voice boomed out clear and sharp, causing everyone to stop and look at him. The younger children came running up, begging him to say something else. He gave them turns speaking into it, to their delight.

Fannie's father stepped into the supervisor's role, walking around and keeping track of the progress, offering suggestions or instructions, sometimes cracking jokes to the crew. He made everyone feel that they had an important job, from the youngest boy swinging a hammer to the oldest man carrying siding.

At midmorning, he called for a break. Noah and his brothers gladly sat down to steaming black coffee, fresh-picked grapes, raisin bars, assorted cookies and tart lemonade. It was beginning to get hot. Noah lifted his wide-brimmed straw hat and wiped the sweat from his brow.

At noon, Fannie began setting out ham and bread for sandwiches. She looked his way and smiled sweetly. He narrowly missed smashing his thumb because he was watching her instead of what he was doing.

As he'd known they would, his mother and sisters-in-law produced a mountain of food in plastic bowls and jars. Along with paper plates and utensils, they placed everything down the center of the folding tables brought out of the school. There were fried chicken, German potato salad, pickles, pickled beets, stacks of brownies, whoopie pies, a jugs of fresh lemonade and a jug of iced tea.

The bishop led the workers in a brief prayer of thanksgiving. Noah's mother made sure everyone had a heaping plate of food on his or her lap before she sat down with a plate of her own. She gazed out over the families gathered together. "It does my heart good to see so many people willing to help."

It did Noah's heart good to see Fannie get her plate of food and leave the group of women for the first time since she'd arrived. He followed her to the swing set beside the school and they each sat down a swing. "Are you enjoying yourself?"

"I am. It almost feels like I'm back in school," she admitted with a shy smile. "Your brothers' wives have some funny stories to share about their husbands, but the bishop's wife takes the cake. If half of what she says is true, he is blessed to have her as his keeper. Twice this month she found his glasses on his mule's rump when he came in from the field."

Noah laughed. "Why there?"

"He claimed it was a handy flat spot to lay them so he could wipe the sweat off of his face, and he just forgot them."

"So mingling hasn't been so bad today?"

She swung gently back and forth. "It hasn't been this morning. Has anyone suggested a ball game later?"

"They have. It will be the annual boys against the men softball game. I will be pitching for the men's team."

"The underdogs?"

"We are not. The opposing pitcher is eleven, but I'm told he has a good arm."

She chuckled. "I can't wait to cheer you on."

"Are you going to be able to come to my regular game tomorrow? It's the last home game of the season. We'll be league champions if we win it and the next away game."

"I do plan to come. Our riding exhibition isn't until next Saturday. Which is good, because we need to practice with our carts. It was a great idea, Noah. I'm glad you thought of it."

It was gratifying that he had pleased her. He wanted to go on making her happy. "If I come up with anything else I'll let you know."

"And I have called you birdbrained for the last time. It was fun while it lasted, but the name doesn't truly fit you."

"Can I walk you home when this is over tonight?"

"I'd like that."

He rose and took her plate. Laying it aside, he said, "I have a little time before I have to get back to work. Would you like a push?"

"Now I really feel like I'm back in school." She giggled as she gripped the chains and lifted her feet.

As the men began their ball game against the boys late in the afternoon, Fannie joined Margret and her sister on a quilt in the shade where they could watch the game in progress. Margret was holding Rebecca's baby on her shoulder. The contented baby was trying to get his entire fist in his mouth and drooling excessively on his fingers.

"He's getting your dress damp," Fannie told her.

"I don't mind. Aren't babies wonderful?"

Fannie wrinkled her nose. "Not if one is drooling down my neck."

Rebecca returned to the quilt and sat down. "I can take him now."

"Is it all right if I hold him a little longer?" Margret asked hopefully.

His mother smiled. "I don't mind."

"He's such a good baby. It must be wonderful to be a mother." Margret patted his back and he burped loudly.

"He is *Gott*'s greatest blessing to me and Samuel. *Gott* willing, you will know the same joy someday."

"I pray you are right, but I'm not getting any younger, and there are many more single women in our community than there are single men because the boys leave as teenagers and don't return."

Lillian called to Rebecca from the school steps. Rebecca waved and rose to her feet again. "If you get tired of holding him, I'm sure Fannie will take him."

"I won't get tired," Margret assured her, smiling at the baby.

"When are you going home?" Fannie asked, desperate to talk about something other than babies. They were cute and they smelled good, but she wasn't ready to want one.

"I leave next week."

"I thought you were staying until the end of the month."

"My sister is staying longer. She has caught the eye of a young man from your church. The only two that struck my fancy are already seeing someone." She gave Fannie a sidelong glance.

Fannie gaped at her in surprise. "Do you mean Noah?"

"Have I offended you?" Margret asked quickly.

"*Nee*, I'm not offended." Surprised, yes, but she wasn't sure why she should be. Noah was a good-looking fellow from a nice family. He was hardworking and kind. Any woman would feel he was good husband material.

"Are you serious about each other?" Margret asked.

Fannie glanced to where Noah was standing in the batter's box as she pondered Margret's question. He was dressed plain today, with dark pants and suspenders over his muscular shoulders. He had taken off his hat in order to run the bases. She liked him best in plain clothes. They suited him. He took a swing at the first pitch and knocked it straight into the second baseman's glove. A groan went up from his bench. He turned to them and held his hands wide. "I'm a pitcher, not a hitter."

Fannie sighed. While she felt her relationship with Noah had grown in recent days, he hadn't said anything to that effect. "I'm afraid I may be more serious about him than he is about me."

"I hope that isn't the case," Margret said softly. "Who is the other fellow?"

"Hiram, but your mother mentioned he is engaged to your sister. It seems I am too late in coming to Bowmans Crossing. The Erb sisters have snagged the best ones."

Fannie caught her lower lip between her teeth. If Noah hadn't been spending so much time with her, would he have discovered he liked the bishop's niece? Had her wild scheme prevented him from finding true romance? Or was he growing to care for her as she had grown to care for him?

Margret glanced Fannie's way. "There is talk that Noah may leave the faith. Are you aware of that?"

"He has not made that decision."

"So you have talked about it? Are you hoping to sway his decision by your affection?"

"*Nee*, I don't feel that would be right."

"And yet you continue to see him, knowing he may leave us."

"He is my friend, and I will support him in his decision."

"I'm surprised to hear you say that. Are you thinking about leaving the faith, as well? If he does?"

"There are many unanswered questions in my heart. If I choose to leave, it will not be because of Noah. What about you? Have you considered leaving?"

"I have already been baptized. I have no intention of leaving the Amish."

"But what if you never marry? What would you do then?"

"I have faith that God has a path laid out for me. I will do my best to accept His will. I long for love, marriage and children of my own, but if that is not to be, I will spend my life in service to my parents, my siblings and my community. There are many things an unmarried woman can do to make life better for all."

"But can you be happy?"

Margret laughed. "Of course I can be happy. Happiness does not come from outside of us. It comes from the inside. My uncle lost both his legs in a farm accident. No one would blame him for descending into bitterness, but he found inner peace and he is as happy as the next person. Perhaps more so, for he knows how close he came to losing his life. I think happiness comes from serving others. I don't think it comes from having the things we think we want."

Fannie glanced to where Noah was playing ball with his brothers. He seemed content today, but she knew questions about his place in the world troubled him. If she hadn't involved him in her courtship ploy, he would have had to end his *rumspringa* and make his decision. Would he have accepted his place among the Amish as God's will without testing his skill as a pitcher? As much as she hated to think of him going out into the world, she knew he needed to find out for himself.

Rebecca came out the school door and stood on the step. "Margret, can you give us a hand? Let Fannie hold Benjamin. It will only take a few minutes. You don't mind, do you, Fannie?"

Before Fannie could form a reply, the drooling baby was thrust into her arms. She sat him upright in her lap, but his head wobbled so much she thought he might hurt his neck. She pulled him close against her chest and cradled him in her arms. He stared at her with wide blue eyes that soon grew worried.

"Don't cry." Fannie searched for something to distract him. She used her bonnet ribbon to dangle in front of him, touching his nose and then pulling it away.

His frown disappeared. He grinned a wide toothless smile when his chubby fingers closed over the ribbon and he promptly stuffed it into his mouth. In a matter of seconds it was wet with drool.

Fannie smiled at him. "At least it's not my neck."

When Margret returned a few minutes later, Fannie reluctantly gave him back. Babies weren't so bad, after all.

"This is the first time in ten years that the grown men have lost to the schoolboy team in their annual game." Noah knew he'd be teased mercilessly when his ball team learned of it.

He sat down on the quilt beside Fannie. Most of the people who had come to the frolic were packing up and heading home. The new wing of the school was finished, except for the siding that needed to be painted, but that would be done by the schoolchildren after the start of the school year. "Timothy and Lillian are tickled with the amount of work that was done today."

When Fannie didn't reply, he glanced her way. She was staring off into the distance. He looked in that direction and saw the bishop helping his wife and nieces into his buggy.

"Margret is a very sweet woman," Fannie said without looking at Noah. "Have you taken the time to visit with her?"

"I'm too busy spending time with you."

"If we weren't dating, would you be interested in her?"

He leaned back on his arms and crossed his legs at the ankles. "If we weren't dating, you'd be in Florida, and I'd be hiding in the barn to avoid all the single women my mother had lined up for me to meet."

"I'm serious."

"Fannie, it's too late now to wonder what would have happened if we had made a different choice. If *Gott* has chosen Margret Stolfus to be my wife, it will come to pass."

"I reckon." She swiveled to face him. "What kind of wife are you looking for?"

"I haven't been looking for a wife, Fannie."

"If you were, what kind of woman would she be?"

"Funny, caring, loyal." *Everything you are.* Only he didn't have the right to say that to her. "What kind of husband are you looking for?"

"If I ever choose to marry, it will be to a man who acccpts me as I am. He won't want to change me. I'll want him to be kind, hardworking and not afraid to say he needs me. I hope that the things I value are important to him, as well."

Noah wasn't sure where this conversation had come from, but he saw Fannie was serious about it. "I reckon I want a woman like my mother. She laughs a lot and she is always trying to feed us.

No matter what troubles arise in our home, she has food to make it better. In my opinion, her cinnamon rolls do the most good."

That coaxed a smile from Fannie. "Oatmeal-raisin cookies are my mother's treatment for what ails us."

"I suspect it's the love that goes in more than the ingredients."

"I'm sure you're right."

Paul came up to them, grinning from ear to ear. "I've just been hired for my first auction."

Noah looked around. "Who would hire you?"

"The *Englisch* nurse. Her brother's charity is holding an auction at the university where he teaches, and their auctioneer just canceled. I've got a job."

"That's *wunderbar*," Fannie said, enjoying his eagerness. "What are they auctioning off and when is it?"

"I don't know. I forgot to ask." He dashed away, leaving Fannie and Noah grinning at each other.

"Are you ready to go home?" Noah held out his hand.

Fannie nodded and allowed him to help her to her feet. Together they folded the quilt and he tucked it under his arm. Side by side, they started toward the road that curved around the school.

His brother Samuel drove by, nodding to them with a knowing smile, but he didn't offer them a lift. Noah tossed the quilt in the back of Samuel's wagon as he went past. He was glad his brother hadn't offered them a ride. Noah wanted to draw out this day with Fannie. He didn't want to hurry it along in the least. She walked as slowly as he did.

"Don't you have ball practice tonight?" She slanted a glance his way.

"It won't hurt me to miss one practice."

"It won't?"

He smiled at her. "Not a bit."

It was twilight by the time they reached the covered bridge. Inside the dark arch, he stopped. Fannie turned toward him. He took her face between his hands. "I'm thinking this might be the right time and the right place, Fannie Erb. Are you busy?"

"Not at all." She closed her eyes and leaned toward him.

He pulled her close and kissed her. Gently at first, but with greater urgency when she responded in kind. The babbling of the river running beneath him, the sounds of the wind and the insects in the reeds all faded away until she was the only thing in his universe.

Any doubts Fannie had about her feelings for Noah vanished at the soft caress of his lips against hers. All she wanted was to move closer and closer still. She slipped her arms around his neck. He pulled her tight against him and held her in a powerful embrace. This wasn't at all like their kiss in the garden. That had been the kiss of a brash boy. This was the kiss of a man.

Her heart was pounding and her head was spinning by the time he drew away, ending the sweetest moment of her life. He didn't release her. He simply tucked her head beneath his chin and held her until his breathing slowed. "You are a remarkable woman, Fannie."

"I'm happy you think so."

"I'd better get you home."

She looked up at him. "Do we have to go?"

"*Ja*, we have to." He laid his arm across her shoulders and started walking with her tucked against his side.

"I'm not going to be busy *all* weekend," she offered.

He chuckled. "I'll keep that in mind."

Fannie walked in silence beside him, unsure what to say. Did this mean anything? Was he ready to remain Amish? Was she? Where did they go from here?

As they reached her lane, a buggy came flying past them.

"Was that Hiram?" Fannie asked, catching a glimpse of the stern-faced young man as he pulled out without acknowledging them.

"I think it was," Noah said.

"I wonder what he was doing at our place?"

"Maybe he's selling your *daed* some pigs."

She chuckled. "Let's go find out."

Before they reached the front door, Fannie saw her mother on the porch, weeping loudly as Fannie's father tried to console her.

"*Mamm*, what's wrong?" Fannie rushed to her side.

"I don't know how I'll ever be able to hold my head up in front of Hiram's family again. I can't believe she would do this to us."

"What are you talking about?" Fannie couldn't make sense of it.

Her father shook his head sadly. "Your sister has broken her engagement to Hiram. He had a letter from her today. She has met someone else in Florida."

Fannie's mother buried her face in her husband's shirtfront. "I never should have sent her to that place."

Chapter Twelve

"I feel terrible. I don't know what to do." The next morning Fannie sat beside Noah on the bench in his mother's flower garden overlooking the river behind his house. She wasn't sure why she had gone to seek him out, but she needed to talk to someone.

"You couldn't know this would happen."

"It was all my idea. Now my sister's life is ruined. Poor Hiram. I can't imagine he will take her back. He must be humiliated. I was always making fun of him the way people made fun of me. How could I be so cruel?"

"I was as cruel in my comments as you were. The saving grace is that Hiram never heard our jests at his expense."

"That doesn't make them right."

"I agree, but all we can do is move forward and behave better in the future. And your sister's life is not ruined. It has taken an unexpected turn, that's all."

"I guess you're right."

"What are your parents going to do about Betsy? Are they sending you to take her place?"

"*Mamm* has gone to the phone shack to put a call through to my grandparents. Their landlady has a phone she lets them use. Once *Mamm* has had a chance to talk to them and to Betsy, she and *Daed* will decide what to do. If they want me to take her place, I will go. I've caused enough trouble for them."

She jumped to her feet and pulled the head off a sunflower. "This was such a simple plan. We both said we weren't hurting anyone. Why did it have to go so wrong? All I was trying to do was help my friend and look what happened."

"I know you're upset, Fannie, but I'd like to talk to you about last night."

He meant the kiss. Was he going to say he was sorry and it never should have happened? She couldn't bear to hear that from him. "I can't, Noah. I can't deal with one more thing." Throwing the crushed yellow petals to the ground, she ran out of the garden and across the field toward home.

At the house, she paused to catch her breath before she went in. Opening the door, she found her mother in the kitchen. Her face was blotchy, but she wasn't crying. Fannie sat in the chair beside her. "What did *Grossmammi* say? Did you speak to Betsy?"

She nodded. "I spoke to your sister."

"Is she coming back?"

"*Nee.* She wishes to remain and continue caring for my mother. She has promised to give prayerful thought to her engagement to Hiram. She has also promised to stop seeing the young man she met there. He is not Amish. I pray she comes to her senses and makes the correct decision."

"She will. She is a *goot* daughter."

Her mother clasped Fannie's hand. "You are my *goot dochtah*. I don't know what I would do without you. All things are by the will of *Gott*, but He is testing me and He is testing Betsy. I pray we may be found worthy of His mercy."

Fannie cringed inwardly at being called the good daughter. "I will do whatever I can to help."

Her mother rose slowly to her feet. "I am going to go lie down for a while."

Fannie had never known her mother to lie down in the middle of the day. "Are you okay?"

"I am weary today and I wish to rest, that's all. We have the big game to go to this afternoon."

"Why don't you skip the game? *Daed* can go by himself."

"We must keep up appearances. It wouldn't do to give people a reason to speculate on what is wrong. I'm sure the news will get around quickly, but perhaps Betsy will come to her senses soon and we can say it was all a misunderstanding. Besides, I know you want to watch Noah play."

"I watched him play ball at the frolic."

"Don't neglect him because of this. I want at least one of my children to be settled."

The front door opened and Anna Bowman came in. "Noah just told me. You poor dear. What can I do?" The two women embraced and Fannie slipped quietly out of the house. Noah had been right to send Anna. She was exactly who her mother needed now.

Later that afternoon, Fannie took a seat beside her father on the wooden bleachers set up along the third baseline. They had convinced Fannie's mother to stay home. She was still bursting into tears at the drop of a hat.

Noah and his team were gathered around their coach inside the wire enclosure that served as their dugout. Noah's team soon took the field and Fannie watched in amazement as Noah threw the ball with incredible precision and speed. This was nothing like the good-natured game she had watched yesterday.

She turned to her father. "Noah is very good, isn't he?"

"I have never seen the like."

"Do you think he could play for a professional team?"

"Maybe. An Amish fellow would have to give up a lot to follow that path. I've only heard of a few who have been good enough to make the major leagues, and that was years ago."

"The *Englisch* players, do they make a lot of money?"

"These fellows? *Nee.* They play for the fun of it. The professionals? I have heard they can earn millions, especially pitchers."

"Millions of dollars for throwing a ball? I should learn how to do it."

Her father laughed. "I wouldn't let your mother hear you say that. It's a shame Noah can't play for a few more years. It sure is nice to have a winning local team for a change."

"Noah could continue playing. I see no reason for him to stop."

"Are you saying you don't plan to wed this fall?"

She stared at her feet. "I'm not ready to marry so soon."

"Your mother gave me cause to think otherwise."

"I'm afraid that is wishful thinking on *Mamm*'s part."

She watched Noah walk in and take the ball from Walter, who met him halfway. They spoke briefly, then Noah returned to the pitcher's mound. Leaning toward her father, she said, "I hope you can explain this to me. I never liked baseball, so I never played. I know about strikes and balls. I know about outs and innings, but why does Noah nod at the batters?"

"He's nodding at the catcher, not the batter. Walter is giving him signals inside his glove for what kind of pitch he wants Noah to throw."

"Noah says Walter is the best catcher in the league."

"I'm not sure about that, but he's their cleanup hitter."

"What's a cleanup hitter?"

He looked at her as if she'd grown another head. "Are you jesting with me?"

"I wouldn't ask if I knew. Help me learn the game. Mother says I have to impress Noah the way she impressed you."

"Her cooking impressed me. A cleanup hitter is the fourth batter in the lineup. The hope is that several of the first three men will be on base when it's the cleanup hitter's turn. He is normally the most powerful hitter on the team and the one most likely to drive in runs."

"I'm sure Noah could be a cleanup hitter, too."

"His batting average is pretty low."

"Is that good?"

"It's okay for a pitcher. They aren't expected to be good hitters."

"I heard him mention that at the frolic."

When the inning was over and Noah's team came in, Fannie listened to the calls coming from the people in the stands. Some were for the players, calling out encouragement. Others were unkind suggestions, mostly made by fans of the visiting team.

Walter drove in two runs when it was his turn to bat, drawing cheers from everyone around her. As Noah approached the plate, Fannie rose to her feet, cupped her hands around her mouth and yelled, "Knock the hide off that thing. Knock it out of the park."

Her father yanked her back to the bench. "Do not be immodest, daughter."

"Everyone else is yelling."

Noah searched the stands and located her. She waved. He walked into the batter's box and struck out. Fannie leaned back on the bench. "That's too bad. He'll do better next time."

He didn't. At least, not when he came up to bat. He got on base twice during the game, but never scored. Although she wasn't certain, his pitching seemed to decline, as well. She continued to call out her encouragement, in spite of her father's ire, but it made no difference. Still, the Fire Eaters won by a single run.

Afterward, she stood and waited for Noah to come out of the fire station. Walter walked by on his way in. He stopped when he caught sight of her and came over. "What did you think of our game?"

"I'm happy you won, but I'm no expert on baseball. Give me a horse and I'll list all his finer points and flaws. Did Noah play well?"

"I wouldn't call this his best game, but we won."

"Why wasn't it his best?"

"Honestly, I think it was because you were here."

"Me? What did I do?"

"I noticed he had a hard time keeping his head in the game. I think he was more interested in seeing what you were doing."

"My father was upset with my behavior, but it's hard not to yell for you men when everyone around me is yelling. I thought it was fun. I'm sorry I haven't been to more games. You are league champions now?"

"Only if we win our next game."

"You must be very pleased."

"It's a step in the right direction."

"Tell Noah I'm waiting for him, will you?" She was eager to see him. She wanted to share what she had learned about her sister's plans and to apologize for running away that morning. She'd chosen to leave rather than to show him her poor temper.

"You know Noah has been thinking about pursuing a professional ball career, don't you?"

She folded her arms over her middle and stared at the ground. "I know that."

"Are you trying to talk him out of it?"

Glancing at Walter's set face, Fannie realized he saw her as a threat to his dreams. "Noah must make his decision without influence from anyone. It is between him and *Gott*."

"He's the best pitcher I've ever seen. Don't let him throw his gift away."

Noah was toweling his hair dry when Walter sat down beside him. The room was full of men congratulating each other and laughing. A coveted title was only one game away. Walter gave him a sidelong glance. "You barely pulled that one out, my friend."

He'd been distracted by a loud redhead in the bleachers yelling his name and making him smile. "I wasn't on my game, that's for sure."

"I noticed." Walter was annoyed.

Noah shrugged. "Anyone can have a bad day."

"You've had an off week. You've never missed a practice before. Want to tell me why you weren't here yesterday?"

"I was at the school frolic." Noah didn't look

at his friend. He could have made the practice if he'd tried.

"Until after dark?"

"I was busy."

"Busy with Fannie." It was a statement, not a question.

Noah smiled, thinking of the kiss on the bridge. "We're getting along pretty well."

"I thought you said it wasn't serious."

"It wasn't."

Walter arched his eyebrow. "But now it is?"

"Have you ever been in love?" Noah looked at his friend.

"No. Are you in love?"

Noah smiled. "I think I am."

"Does this mean you are ready to give up ball? If you are, I need to know. I have a lot riding on the next game and the state tournament if we get invited. This may be my only shot. If you can't help me get where I need to go, you have to tell me now. Don't leave me hanging."

Was he ready to give up ball? Noah realized if he wanted a life with Fannie, he would have to do just that.

No, he was getting ahead of himself. One kiss, no matter how wonderful, didn't mean Fannie wanted a life with him. She had her own dreams and her own decisions to make.

Yet even the remote possibility of spending a

lifetime with her had him thinking twice about what it was that he really wanted.

"What's it going to be?" Walter asked.

Noah shook his head. "I won't leave you hanging."

"I hope not. We have been friends a long time. We've been through a lot together. You know how important this is to me. I thought it was just as important to you."

"I had an off night, but we won. As for the state tournament, it is up to the tournament committee to invite the teams they want to see matched up. Our success or our failure is up to *Gott*."

"I believe that just as you do, but my dad has a favorite Amish proverb he likes to quote. *All that you do, do with your might. Things done by halves are never done right.* Don't go after the next game halfheartedly or it's over. For all of us."

Walter was right. Noah had become so involved with Fannie's group, and with her, that he was neglecting the men who depended on him. It wasn't just a game to them, especially Walter. It was much more to him. Noah scanned the room. The honor of the fire company and the community was riding on the outcome of this season.

"I will heed your words and make sure that I pitch with all my might."

Walter patted his shoulder. "Thanks. Fannie

seems like a sweet gal. She'll still be here when the season is over."

Would she? Or would she be on her way to Florida? He needed to see her.

She was waiting for him when he stepped outside, and his heart grew light at the sight of her smiling face.

He reached for her hand and she laced her fingers with his. "I had planned to ride with Walter, but would you like to walk home with me?"

"I would."

"Did you enjoy the game?"

She chuckled. "Couldn't you tell? My father was upset with me for my immodest behavior."

"I liked your behavior."

She pressed a hand to her chest. "I'm shocked."

"Why?"

"You have actually found something you like about me and you admitted it."

"A minor lapse of judgment."

She yanked her hand away. "I thought so."

He snatched it back. "I'm kidding. I like lots of things about you, Fannie."

She rolled her eyes. "Now you're kidding me."

"Nope, not even a little. A vain woman would ask me to list them."

He watched the indecision narrow her eyes, but then she shook her head. "I won't rise to your bait."

"You don't trust me?"

"I do. About as far as I can throw you."

He laughed. "I like that you aren't a vain woman."

And I like almost everything about you, she thought as he walked beside her. Each day her affection for him deepened.

"What did you find out about your sister?"

"*Mamm* spoke to her. She's reconsidering her decision to break her engagement, and she has promised not to see the man who prompted her choice. I won't be going to Florida. Betsy will be staying for a while."

"I'm glad of that."

"Me, too."

It was comfortable walking with him, hand in hand. The sun was a red ball hanging low in the west as it sank behind them. It cast their long shadows down the road in front of them. Fannie could remember her grandparents walking this way in the evenings. What would it be like to spend a lifetime holding Noah's hand?

"Fannie, what are we going to do about this courtship?"

"I have been wondering that, too. I hate to break it off now. My mother will be crushed."

"What if we don't break it off?"

Her heart tripped in her chest, causing her to catch her breath. "What are you suggesting?"

"We're getting along well, don't you think?"

"Surprisingly well, actually."

He chuckled. "I knew you were going to say that. Let's give it some more time. Let's make it a real courtship. What do you say?"

If she agreed, would he remain Amish? Would she be asking him to throw away his gift from God as Walter had suggested?

She bit the corner of her lip as she struggled to find the right thing to say.

Chapter Thirteen

On Wednesday afternoon, Fannie sat on Trinket, ready to lead her group through their program, but all she could think about was Noah's request to make their courtship a real one. Instead of saying yes, she had asked for some time to think it over. It was the memory of the disappointment that had flashed across his face that was keeping her up at night.

She told herself there was no harm in waiting, but she hadn't believed there was harm in her idea in the first place. That had been a false assumption. Fannie wasn't eager to create another set of problems.

Trinket shifted her weight, eager to get started. Their arena was an open field marked with reflective orange tape on thin metal rods, the kind used to hold electric fence wires. Hundreds of Amish folk were lined up behind the barrier, waiting for the draft horse auction to begin. Fannie and Connie had placed orange cones to mark the perimeter of their patterns so the girls didn't feel lost in the large area.

A heavyset man wearing an orange vest over his blue shirt came up to her. "Are you ready to begin?"

She nodded and rode over to where Zoe and Connie had the speaker system plugged in to a long extension cord. "It's showtime."

Riding back, she took her place and waited for the music to begin. The rollicking strains of the song began and Fannie said, "Now."

Because she was the first rider, she had no idea if the others were in line behind her until she made the first turn. She glanced back and smiled. The horses were in near-perfect step as they cantered across the field. Waiting for the pause in the singer's voice at just the right spot, Fannie wheeled Trinket left. The line of riders split four abreast, going in opposite directions with awesome precision. A few seconds later, the music stopped abruptly.

Fannie looked in Connie's direction. A tall man in a dark hat and suit with a long, shaggy gray beard was walking onto the field. He motioned to Abbie and Laura, who rode slowly to him. Fannie cantered over, too.

He sliced the air with one finger. "This is not

permitted. *Dess* music of the *Englisch* is verboten. *Kumma.*" He turned on his heel and walked away.

Fannie looked to Abbie and Laura for an explanation, although she suspected she already knew the answer. Timothy came out to stand with the group. "What's going on?"

Laura looked ready to cry. "That's our grandpa. He is the bishop of our church. I'm sorry, Fannie. We have to go."

"Of course. Don't worry about it." She managed to smile at them, but inside she was seething.

She rode to Connie and motioned for the others to join her. "Start the music over. We'll finish with six."

Noah watched Fannie pacing across Timothy's kitchen and wondered if the floor would have a groove in it when she was done. He'd seen her angry, but not quite like this. "He just walked out and stopped our performance yesterday. His granddaughters were humiliated."

"He was doing what he believed was right," Lillian said.

"The girls hadn't told their family that they were riding to recorded music," Timothy added. "They thought if it was okay for the others, it was okay for them. However, Bishop Lapp leads a very conservative church, and even for unbaptized members, music is forbidden. I spoke to the man at length and he won't be swayed on this."

"So, this project is dead," Connie said glumly.

"Not necessarily," Lillian said. "Timothy, tell them."

"Lillian asked Debra Merrick to do some research for me and she came up with an alternative. She showed us a video of an Amish drill team where the leader signaled changes with a whistle. I spoke with Bishop Lapp this morning and he finds this acceptable."

Fannie stopped pacing. "A whistle instead of music. It won't work."

"Why not, Fannie?" Noah asked.

"All of us, including the horses are keyed into the beat. We don't have time to relearn our timing and signals. The Horse Expo is two weeks away."

Connie clasped her hands together on the red-and-white-checkered tablecloth. "What choice do we have? I had to prepay to reserve the hauler and motel rooms for us. I might get a refund on some of it, but not all of it."

Fannie moved to stare out the window. "Cut your losses and run, Connie. I'm sorry I ever got you into this."

Connie moved to put her arm around Fannie. "It was a fine idea. We've simply run into a stumbling block."

"Another one. What next?" She shrugged off Connie's arm and went outside.

Noah followed her. "Don't give up. You and your crew can do it. I have faith in you."

"I don't have faith in me anymore."

"Let me take you home." She was hurting and he had no idea how to help her.

"I'm sorry, Noah. I'd rather be alone." She paused. "I forgot to ask. Did you win your last game?"

"We did. We're the league champions."

"That's great. I guess I can give the whistle thing a try." She mounted her horse and rode away, leaving him aching to hold her and comfort her. Ever since he had asked to make their courtship real, she had been pulling away from him. Was it because she knew he might not remain Amish, or was it something else?

The members of Noah's ball team crowded into Eric's office and waited. The coaches of the teams that were being invited to the state tournament were to be notified by phone after ten o'clock on Thursday morning. It was ten fifteen.

"They aren't going to call." Walter pushed out of his chair and moved to the window.

"Have faith. We won our league." Noah, too, was beginning to doubt they would be contacted.

Teams qualified for the invitational by participating in regional tournaments held throughout the state. While finishing in the top generally guaranteed an invitation, it was up to the State Baseball Federation to determine invitees.

"There will be twelve teams in all. It takes time to call everyone." Eric drummed his fingers on his desk beside his smartphone.

"I need some air." Walter pushed past Noah and went outside.

Noah followed his friend. "Waiting is the hard part."

"Not playing will be the hard part."

"If we don't get called, there is always next year."

"You won't be pitching for us next year. Without your talent, we are only slightly above average players."

"That's not true."

"Isn't it?"

"What makes you think I won't be pitching again next year?"

"The girl."

Noah stared at his shoes. "I'm not sure I'm what she wants."

"But she is what *you* want."

"I'm trying to discover God's will for me. Is it Fannie? Is it a professional ball career? If that doesn't work out, will I come home and remain

Amish because I've failed or because God wants me here? He has to show me the way."

Walter sighed. "Noah, maybe God wants you to make the choice. Did you ever think of that?"

Noah was saved from answering when he heard the sound of Eric's cell phone ringing. He and Walter grinned at each other and hurried back inside. Eric picked up the phone and listened. He gave them the thumbs-up sign and everyone cheered.

Noah slapped Walter on the back. "See? Faith."

"I can't believe it. This is my shot, Noah. I feel it in my bones."

"I pray you are right."

Eric stood. "Everyone is invited to my place for pizza. We need to celebrate."

The laughing group of men piled out of the office into the main bay of the fire station. Someone started honking the fire engine's horn.

Noah watched his teammates congratulating each other and realized there was only one person he wanted to share the news with as soon as possible. Fannie would be at her practice. He tapped Walter on the arm. "Can you run me over to Connie Stroud's farm before you go get pizza?"

"Aren't you coming with us?"

"I'll be over later. Save me a slice."

"Sure. Hop in."

Ten minutes later, Walter dropped Noah in

front of Connie's barn. Noah entered the building and leaned on the rail. The team was lined up by twos. Fannie blew a whistle once and started forward. They were only a few paces along when Susan came up too quickly and had to pull back. Rose bumped into her and Goldenrod turned to the outside, breaking the pattern.

Rose got her horse back in line as Fannie blew the whistle and started to circle left. Sylvia had been holding back to let Rose regain her position. She turned too short and cut in front of Abbie. The resulting confusion made everyone stop.

Fannie whirled Trinket around and threw down her whistle. "This isn't going to work."

Noah stepped into the ring. "What's going on here?"

"What does it look like? We're riding without music and making mistake after mistake," Fannie snapped.

Sylvia looked ready to cry. Abbie and Laura were sniffling.

"We are learning to make our pattern changes when I blow the whistle, only we can't get it right." Fannie's voice shook with frustration.

He crossed to Fannie's side. "I'm sorry. Where is Timothy?"

"He's talking to Connie about where the girls should stay in Columbus. They are trying to find someplace less expensive and figure out how we are going to get the carts there."

"It turns out I'll be in Columbus at the same time you'll be there."

"Your team got the invitation?"

"We did."

She rolled her eyes. "You must be so thrilled. It's all working out exactly as you planned."

He pulled back. "You don't sound thrilled for me."

"Am I supposed to be?"

"I thought so. I thought you'd be happy for me. Maybe I was mistaken in your feelings."

"I guess you were. At least this stupid fake courtship can be over now. I can't tell you how happy that makes me."

"Fannie, I know you're upset, but don't take it out on me." He picked up the whistle. "It's going to take more time, that's all. You'll get it."

"We don't have more time. We've only got two weeks."

He handed her the whistle. "Everyone here will try their best. Stop being a baby about it and do the work."

She knocked the whistle from his hand. "That's easy for you to say. You won your season. You'll be pitching in the tournament of your dreams. I'm sure you'll be laughing at us as we make fools of ourselves in front of a thousand people.

All our hard work will be for nothing. Connie will have wasted the money she's already spent on entry fees and motel rooms for us. I wish I'd never come up with this stupid idea, and I wish you'd leave me alone."

She kicked Trinket into a gallop and shot out the arena door.

Noah started after her, but Susan touched his arm. "Let her go. Let her blow off some steam."

"You girls are looking to her for leadership."

"And that's why she'll be back when she cools down," Susan said with a tiny smile.

He sighed. "You're right. I reckon she has to figure that out for herself."

The side door flew open and Zoe came running in. She gripped the railing, her eyes wide and frightened. "Come quick."

Noah started toward her. "What is it?"

"Fannie tried to jump Trinket over the south fence and they fell. I think she's hurt bad."

Noah vaulted over the railing and raced out the door. Fannie was lying facedown in the grass just beyond the smashed board fence. Trinket lay a few feet away from her. He sprinted toward Fannie. *Please, Lord, let her be all right.*

Sliding to a stop beside her, Noah dropped to his knees as his first-aid training took over. There was blood on the side of her head and face, but she was breathing. Relief surged through his body and he started breathing again, too. He gently took her wrist in his hand to check her pulse. It was erratic but strong. *Thank You, God.*

He still didn't know how badly injured she might be, but he knew enough not to move her. Trinket was struggling to get up but couldn't. Blood covered her neck and front legs.

Connie arrived beside Noah. "How bad is it?"

"I'm not sure." He leaned down. "Fannie, can you hear me? Speak to me, Fannie."

"Trinket?" Her voice was a bare whisper, but it was the sweetest sound he'd ever heard.

"I'll take care of her," Connie said, moving to the horse. Speaking softly, she eased the mare's head back to the ground to keep her from moving. She quieted and lay with her sides heaving.

Connie pulled her cell phone from her pocket. "I'm calling 911."

"I'm so sorry," Fannie whispered. She closed her fingers over Noah's hand.

"Where are you hurt, *liebchen*?"

"I can't move—my legs." Her fingers went limp.

Noah squeezed them tighter. "Fannie, Fannie stay with me."

She didn't respond. *Please, God, don't take her from me. Not now, not before I've told her how much I love her.*

He leaned close and kissed her pale cheek. "I love you, Fannie. Do you hear me? I love you."

She had only herself to blame.

Her foolish, childish temper tantrum had cost her dearly.

Fannie lay inside the MRI machine at the hospital, listening to the thudding sounds it made. The doctor had explained that it would take detailed images of her spine and show what was wrong. It would tell them if she would walk again.

She was afraid to pray for herself. Afraid it was too late to ask God to heal her, but she prayed He would spare Trinket. Her poor, brave horse had done everything Fannie had asked and received only pain as a reward.

Fannie didn't remember anything after flying over Trinket's head until she woke up being wheeled into the emergency entrance of the hospital. She tried to look for Noah, but she couldn't move her head. Then she heard his voice telling her to lie still. The rest of her admission was a blur of bits and pieces, until now.

Finally, the hammering sound stopped and someone spoke to her from the end of the tunnel she lay in. Her bed moved backward, bringing her into the bright lights of the imaging room. She couldn't turn her head away from their glare. A hard plastic collar around her neck prevented any movement. She closed her eyes as she was wheeled out. When her bed stopped moving, she swallowed against the pain the jolt caused in her back.

"We are here, Fannie." Her mother's voice made Fannie open her eyes again. Her parents were bending over her. There were tears in their eyes.

"Don't worry, *Mamm*. I'm fine." Fannie smiled to prove her point, but neither parent look relieved. "How is Trinket?"

Her father laid a hand on her head. "Noah told us Connie is taking care of her. The vet was on his way. As soon as Connie knows something for sure, she will call Noah and he will tell you. You are not to worry about your horse now. You are to get well."

The young doctor she had seen earlier came up to the other side of her bed. "I'm happy to say she is going to do just that if she takes it easy and does as we tell her."

"She will walk again?" Fresh tears poured down her mother's face.

"She has two burst-fractured vertebrae, but her spinal cord is intact. The bones are cracked, but none of the pieces are displaced. She won't need surgery. Her paralysis is most likely caused by what we call spinal shock. It can last a few hours to a few weeks after an injury like this. We are giving her anti-inflammatory medicine to relieve the tissue swelling and pressure. Other than a nasty concussion, we didn't find anything else abnormal. Fannie, can you wiggle your toes for me?"

She concentrated and moved her left foot a fraction.

"Good. The steroids are already helping. You are a very fortunate young woman. Our physical therapy department will fit you with a back brace that must be worn at all times while the bones mend."

"Will I be able to ride again?" Fannie whispered.

"Not for several months, but eventually, yes. I suggest you avoid having your horse step on your back in the future."

"Is that what happened? I don't remember. Trinket would never hurt me on purpose."

"I'm a horseman myself, so I believe you. I'm having the nurse give you something to help you rest. We will move you to a regular room when one is available. Expect to stay with us for at least three days. I know the Amish don't believe in medical insurance, so I will get you home as soon as I can."

The nurse came in and injected something into

Fannie's IV. "This is going to make you sleepy very quickly."

Fannie's father held out his hand. "*Danki, Herr Doktor.* We are deeply grateful to you."

The doctor shook his hand. "I did my part, but God was looking after her."

When the man left the room, Fannie's mother leaned down to kiss her brow. "We are so thankful. Noah is waiting outside. Shall I have him come in?"

Shame blossomed in Fannie's heart. She remembered the cruel words she'd spoken to Noah. None of it was true. Yet God in His mercy had spared her life after all the deceit she had carried out. It was time to make a clean breast of it.

"*Mamm*, I have to tell you something first and I don't want you to be angry with Noah. He thought he was helping me."

Her parents exchanged puzzled glances.

"What are you talking about?" her mother asked.

"Noah and I are not courting. We never were. We made up the story so I could stay and ride in the drill team instead of going to Florida. I truly wanted to help Connie, but that doesn't change the fact that what I did was wrong."

"You lied to us?" Her mother drew back.

"I did. Please forgive me."

Her father's brow darkened. "And Noah lied to his family about this, too?"

"Yes," she answered softly, ashamed that she had suggested the scheme in the first place and had to lay any part of the blame at his door. "I'm so sorry."

"We will speak of this again when you are home." Her father put his arm around her mother's shoulders.

There was a knock at the door and Noah looked in. Relief filled his eyes. "You're awake."

"Come in." Fannie blinked and had trouble focusing on his dear face. She had so much to atone for.

"The doctor said it's good news. You're going to be fine," Noah said.

"Noah, I had to tell them."

He stepped inside. "Tell them what?"

"That we aren't courting. That we made it up."

"Fannie, I need to talk to you about us." He looked at her parents. "It's not what you think."

"I know how upset your mother will be and I am ashamed of my daughter's part in this." Fannie heard the disapproval in her mother's voice, but she couldn't keep her eyes open any longer. "I'm sorry, Noah, but now you are free."

He didn't want to be free.

The door opened behind Noah and a nurse

came in. "We have a room for her now. If you'll wait outside for a few minutes while we get her ready, you can follow us when we leave."

Noah longed to tell Fannie his true feelings, but she was already asleep. He would have to wait. He held the door for Fannie's parents and felt their disapproval as they passed. Outside in the hall, they turned to him. He wanted Fannie to hear his words first, but it was her parents who needed to know his intentions now.

He took a deep breath. "What Fannie has told you is the truth, but it isn't the whole truth. I agreed to a pretend courtship because my parents were pressuring me to stop playing ball, join the faith and take a wife. I wasn't ready for that."

"I can't believe the two of you have deceived us this way." Belinda dabbed at her eyes with her handkerchief.

"It was wrong and I beg your forgiveness. But I want you to know my feelings for Fannie have changed. I am in love with your daughter. I kept up the pretense of a courtship because I wanted to be with her, not because I needed to convince you or my parents of my continued affections. I love her, and I pray that she loves me."

Ernest stroked his beard. "You aren't certain of my daughter's feelings?"

"Fannie and I quarreled before her accident. We both said hurtful things. You know her temper. I'm not sure she will believe me when I tell her how I truly feel."

Belinda gave him a watery smile. "Fannie is quick to anger and often speaks in haste, but I have seen a change in her recently. I believe it is because she has come to care for you, too, Noah, but Fannie can't be pushed into anything. She only digs in her heels."

The door to Fannie's room opened and two nurses wheeled her bed into the hall. Noah stood back to let them pass. He gently touched Fannie's shoulder, but she didn't open her eyes. One of the nurses said, "We are moving her to room 211. You can follow us, if you like."

They started down the hall with Belinda walking behind them. Ernest laid a hand on Noah's shoulder. "Fannie is a lot like my Belinda was when I first met her. Sassy, full of vinegar and determined to be independent. Like her mother, my daughter can be led, but she can't be driven. You have your work cut out for you."

"She is worth it. I can't imagine my life without her."

Chapter Fourteen

Fannie woke in near-total darkness. It took her a long moment to realize where she was. A faint light showed through the blinds covering a window beside her bed. The pain in her back was a dull ache. She lay still, not wanting to rouse it, and rubbed her sleep-blurry eyes with the heels of her hands. The hard collar was gone from her neck, but another brace encased her body from her chest to her hips. It was a pointed reminder of her foolishness and of God's mercy.

She had hurt a great many people with her bullheaded determination. Connie had invested her slim resources in Fannie's plan because Fannie convinced her she could make it work. She had lied to her parents and to Noah's family. She had turned her back on her responsibility to her grandparents, sending Betsy to care for them instead. When had horses become more important than her family? More important than her faith?

Shame sent her spirits lower. "I have learned my lesson, Lord," she whispered into the darkness.

Her path forward was clear now. She would beg the forgiveness of those she had wronged. She would strive to undo the hurt she had caused and humbly accept the physical burden of pain God had visited on her. But the pain in her body was nothing compared to the pain in her heart.

She loved Noah. Loved him enough to know that she was the wrong woman for him. He deserved someone better. She was barely trustworthy. She wasn't humble or meek of spirit. She was prideful and arrogant. Instead of turning to God for help, she had assumed she could supply the answers and win the day by herself. Noah did, indeed, deserve a better woman, and she would make sure she never hurt him again.

It was almost noon the next day when Noah returned to the hospital. He wanted to see Fannie alone. He needed to tell her how much he loved her.

The door to her room was open. He stopped just outside. Connie, Zoe and all the girls from the team were gathered around Fannie's bed.

"The girls don't think they can do this without you, Fannie. You're the leader," Connie said.

"I'm a poor leader. My actions yesterday were childish and irresponsible. I don't think you can do this without me. I *know* you can do it. Zoe, you have the routine down as well as I do and you're a better rider. If you don't mind dressing plain, Zoe, you will be a *wunderbar* addition to The Amish Girls."

"You want me to wear a bonnet? Isn't that against the rules or something?"

"I will loan you one of my *kapps,*" Abbie said.

"You can wear one of my dresses over your riding clothes. No one will know you aren't Amish," Laura said with a giggle.

Zoe glanced around the room. "I don't feel right about pretending to be Amish."

Fannie reached toward her and took her hand. "You're right, Zoe. You should never pretend to be something you aren't."

Abbie put an arm around her friend. "My *mamm* can make you a shirt out of the same material as our pink dresses. You can wear a white kerchief over your hair. That way you'll still match us, but folks will know you're *Englisch.*"

Connie leaned down to her daughter. "Is that acceptable?"

"It sure is." Zoe nodded vigorously, clearly happy to be part of the group.

Fannie smiled at them. "I'm sorry I won't be there to help you practice. Susan, I want you to take over as the group leader. Timothy says he can supervise you six days a week, if that's what it will take."

"We won't let you down," Susan promised. The other girls all agreed.

"I know you will do your best. That's all anyone can do. Getting frustrated and angry won't help." She rapped on the brace encasing her upper body. "I know. I tried it and look where it got me. Ask *Gott* for help as often as you need it. He is listening."

"Why was *Gott* so unfair to you?" Pamela asked, a catch in her voice.

Fannie reached out to cup the child's face. "We can't know why bad things happen, but *Gott* has a reason. I believe He had a lesson for me to learn. My biggest mistake was not putting *Gott* first in my life. I didn't pray for guidance when I told Connie my idea for a drill team, not even when new problems arose. I thought I had to do it myself. I had to make it work. Worst of all, I didn't give thanks for you, my friends. I have been greatly blessed and I failed to be grateful." Her voice trembled and tears filled her eyes.

Connie laid her hand over Fannie's. "We should go, honey. You need your rest."

"How is Trinket?" Fannie asked quickly, wiping her cheek with the back of her hand.

"Trinket is recovering nicely. Fortunately, she didn't sustain any broken bones, just some deep cuts and bad bruises. Don't worry about her. We are taking good care of her, aren't we girls?"

"Very *goot* care," Zoe said in a bad Amish accent.

Noah stepped back as the girls left Fannie's room and thanked them for coming. They were being brave for Fannie's benefit, but he could see how upset they were.

Connie stayed beside him as the girls walked on. "I know she has been through a lot, but I'm worried about her. Keep an eye on her, will you?"

"She sounded fine to me."

Connie didn't look convinced. "I agree she said all the right things, but the fire in her eyes is missing."

"Don't fret. Fannie is a strong woman. She will bounce back from this."

"I hope you're right."

He dismissed her worry and opened the door to Fannie's room. "May I come in?"

"Hello, Noah." She smiled at him, but it didn't reach her eyes. She looked down at her hands clasped together on her brace.

"I'm glad to see you looking better. You gave me a terrible fright."

"I'm sorry for that." Why wouldn't she look at him?

He pulled a chair up beside her bed. "Fannie, I want to talk to you about us."

"It's a relief to stop pretending, isn't it? I feel like I've had a boulder lifted off my chest."

"That's just it. I'm not pretending any more, Fannie. I'm in love with you."

She looked at him then, with sadness in her eyes. "I've come to care for you, too, Noah, but not in that way. I care for you as a friend. I always will, but we must go our separate ways now."

"Nee." Noah couldn't believe what he was hearing. His heart sank at the blankness of her expression.

Fannie saw the confusion on Noah's face and hardened her heart against comforting him. She had done him a great disservice. He thought he was in love with her, but it was only pity and he would realize that soon enough. He deserved a better woman than she could ever be. "You aren't responsible for what happened, Noah. This was *Gott*'s will."

He shook his head. "I kissed you, Fannie, and you kissed me back. That wasn't the kiss of a friend."

"I'm sorry, Noah. I never intended to hurt you.

I wanted our courtship to become real. Every time someone mentioned it, I was ashamed of what I had done. I was ashamed of making you a party to my deception."

"We started out together for the wrong reasons, but that doesn't matter now. I love you, Fannie. Nothing you say will change that."

"Then I have done you an even greater disservice than I imagined. Please forgive me."

He scooted his chair back. "You're tired. You're in pain. I should have waited until you were feeling better before I said anything."

"Please leave, Noah." She looked out the window.

"We can talk about this later. Don't shut me out, Fannie," he pleaded.

"When I'm recovered enough to travel, I'll be going to Florida and Betsy will be returning. I have neglected my duty to my grandparents. I see that now."

"What about Trinket? What about your friends?"

She stared at her clenched fingers. "My father will take care of my horse. I have caused Connie enough trouble. The Amish Girls will ride without me and they will be fine."

"What about me, Fannie? How can I be fine if you can't even look at me?"

She forced herself to smile at him. "You had

a purpose for joining me in our false courtship. That purpose still exists. *Gott* has given me an answer to my prayers. I accept it, even if it isn't the answer I wanted. I will take my vows when I return from Florida. You must find *Gott*'s answer for your life. Go to the state tournament and use the gift He has given you. To do less than your best would be wrong. If it is His will that you leave us and play professional ball, He will tell you."

"And if it is His will that I come home?"

"Either way, I will be happy for you, Noah. I will always be your friend."

"Fannie, I don't understand. I have come to know you and admire you, and I thought you returned my feelings."

"I admire your kindness. I admire many things about you, Noah, but I'm not the woman you need."

"I will be the judge of that."

He wasn't leaving. If he didn't go, she would break down and tell him she loved him. She closed her eyes. "After prayerful consideration, I realize you are not the man for me. I'm sorry. I'm very tired. Please go now." She turned her face toward the window, unwilling to watch him walk out of her life. When she heard the door close, tears streamed down her cheeks.

"Goodbye, Noah. I love you, too," she whispered.

* * *

Eric Swanson had been kind enough to take Noah to the hospital and then home. Noah didn't share any of his conversation with Fannie on the ride, but he was sure Eric knew he was upset. When they reached the farm, Noah stepped out of the car and looked back at him. "Would you like to come in?"

"Another time. Are you okay?"

"We'll see."

"Hang in there. She's going to be fine."

Noah nodded. Fannie was going to be fine, but he wasn't.

He found his mother in the kitchen when he entered the house. He had confessed his part in Fannie's fake courtship to his parents the night before. They had been shocked and dismayed by his behavior, but they forgave him and listened to the whole story without harsh judgment.

His mother pulled a pan of cinnamon rolls from the oven. Setting them on the table, she looked at him. "How is she?"

"She's okay." He took a seat at the table.

"And how are you?"

He raked his hands through his hair. "I don't know. I love her, but she says she doesn't love me. Where does that leave me?"

"Fannie has had a terrible experience, Noah.

Give her time to heal. She will see things more clearly in time."

"I hope you are right." He pulled off a piece of cinnamon bun and popped it into his mouth. It burned, but he welcomed the pain. It took his mind off the ache in his heart.

His mother moved the pan away from him. "You never could wait for the frosting."

"I like them plain." He watched her make her glaze from powdered sugar, butter, vanilla and hot water.

"I like mine sweet and gooey." She stirred the mixture rapidly.

"*Mamm*, what would you do if I didn't join the church?"

"I'd never make you cinnamon rolls again," she said, without missing a stroke.

"I'm serious."

She stopped stirring to stare at him with deep concern in her eyes. "Are you actually considering this?"

"Maybe. I'm not sure."

She set her bowl down and took a seat across from him. "I would be brokenhearted, but I would accept your decision if that is what *Gott* wills for you. We must each serve Him in our own way."

He gave vent to his frustration. "How can I tell

what His will is? I'm waiting for a sign, something to tell me what He wants from me. Am I to be a baseball player or a farmer? English or Amish? How do I know?"

Her expression softened. "My son, our Lord has given his children a great and terrible gift. The gift of free will. We get to choose our path. When we seek direction in our lives, we must pray for *Gott*'s guidance. But don't expect Him to put up a billboard that says This Way, Noah."

"It would sure be easier if He did."

She leaned forward and placed her hand on his chest. "*Gott*'s answer comes here, not to our eyes or our ears. Listen with your heart and you shall know His will."

Leaning back, she took up her bowl and spread some of the icing over a bun. She pulled it from the pan and broke it in two, offering Noah half. He took it and bit into the sweet, warm bread. "It's *goot. Danki.*"

"I learned a long time ago that *goot* advice goes down more easily with *goot* food. Have I helped you?"

He licked his fingers and nodded. His heart told him Fannie was the only one for him. He hadn't known that right away, but gradually he'd come to realize how much he loved her. Perhaps that was the way God would make known the path he was to choose.

* * *

"Noah is here to see you, Fannie." Her mother stood in the doorway to Fannie's room. Fannie sat in a rocker in the corner of her bedroom, looking out the window. She had been home for a week. Each day Noah had come to visit and each day she had sent him away, but it was becoming harder to do. She missed him so much.

"I don't want to see him. Tell him to stop coming." It hurt to say those words, but a clean break would be better for both of them instead of this painfully drawn-out process.

"As you wish." Her mother closed the door leaving Fannie alone. She blinked back tears and refused to let them fall.

Her door opened again, but it was her father this time. He stood staring at her with his arms crossed over his chest. "Aren't you done feeling sorry for yourself yet?"

She turned her face away. "I'm not feeling sorry for myself. My back aches, and I don't want company."

"Well, you are going to have my company until you agree to leave this room."

"I won't see him."

"He's not here. He and his team are on their way to Columbus. He left with his tail tucked between his legs like a scolded dog. Shame on you for treating him so. The boy is in love with you."

"He'll get over it, and he'll find someone better."

"Do you mean to say my daughter isn't good enough for him?"

"*Nee*, I'm not," she answered in a small voice, wishing her father would go away.

He came across the room and sat on the edge of her bed. "I can see that for myself. Noah deserves a woman with spunk. He needs a sassy gal to make him laugh and show him how wonderful love can be. He doesn't need a damp dishcloth of a woman like you."

"I'm not a damp dishcloth," she snapped back.

"Then stop acting like one. You made some mistakes. Welcome to life. We all make mistakes. Don't compound them by making things worse. That boy loves you. If we can forgive you, why can't you forgive yourself?"

"I don't deserve him."

"I see now. Your pride is getting in the way." He spread his arms wide. "Your sins are too great to be forgiven. Woe to Fannie Erb. Her heart is black as night. No one may love her."

"Don't make fun of me." He was beginning to annoy her.

"Someone should. Poor little Fannie fell off her horse and hurt her back. She can't ride, she can barely walk and she can't be nice to people who care about her. I love you, child, but I am more ashamed of you now than I have ever been in my life."

"What do you want me to do?" she shouted, then covered her mouth with her hand.

He stood. "The Horse Expo is the day after tomorrow and you are going. The doctor says you can travel."

She bit her lip. "They don't need me there."

He shook his head. "This isn't about you. It's about them. They want you there, Fannie. Doing something for someone else is the first step in your recovery. What do you say?"

He was right. It wasn't about her. Not anymore. She nodded. "They deserve my support. I'll go."

Her father came and took her face between his strong, calloused hands. "*Goot.* Noah deserves your support, too, Fannie. He's hurting. He doesn't deserve someone better. Do you know what he does deserve?"

"What?" Tears slipped from the corners of her eyes.

"Someone who loves him as much as you do." Her father kissed her forehead and left her room.

Fannie wiped her damp cheeks. Her father was right. She still hadn't learned her lesson. Instead of praying for God's guidance, she had assumed she knew best and had pushed Noah away. He had gone to his tournament and he might never come back. She bowed her head. "I'm sorry,

Lord. I accept Your forgiveness and I pray it is not too late for me to tell Noah how much I love him. Please bring him back to us."

Chapter Fifteen

Noah stood lined up with his teammates in front of their dugout on the first baseline. The stadium wasn't full, but it held more people that he'd played in front of in his entire life.

"Don't be nervous. Keep your mind on the game," Walter said, a trickle of sweat slipping down his temple.

"I'm not the one who is nervous." Noah wasn't. There wasn't anything at stake for him. He scuffed the white chalk line with the toe of his cleats. If a minor-or major-league ball team recruited him, fine. There was little reason to go home. Fannie wouldn't even see him. How could he live across the road from her knowing she didn't want him when he loved her more with every breath he took?

"How is she?" Walter asked, looking his way. Noah knew he was referring to Fannie. Everyone on the team had heard about the accident. "Home and mending, my mother tells me. Her drill team is performing at the Horse Expo across town tonight. I plan to get over there after our game and watch them. It's the least I can do."

Timothy had kept him informed of the group's progress. They were doing well using just the whistle, but they still missed their music. They were all worried about performing in front of such a large crowd. The event had been Fannie's dream. He hoped she would be there to see it, too. And he hoped he would have a chance to see her.

He hadn't spoken to Fannie since that day at the hospital. He'd stopped by her home daily, but she'd refused to see him. Her mother was apologetic, but Fannie wouldn't budge. She didn't want him. He was trying to accept that.

The game announcer's voice came over the PA system. "Please rise for our national anthem."

The crowd surged to its feet. A young woman walked to the pitcher's mound and began to sing. Her voice soared over the air in pure, clear notes without accompaniment. When the last word of the song faded away, applause burst from the crowd.

Walter clapped wildly. "The girl has some pipes. That's a tough song to sing a cappella."

Noah glanced to where nearly fifty members of his extended family and people from his community were seated together behind the dugout, eager to watch their hometown team play. Even Bishop Beachy was in attendance, although his wife wasn't. They had rented a bus to bring them all this way and they planned to travel to the horse show after the baseball game. Their plain dark clothes, white bonnets and straw hats made them stand out sharply from the colorful people around them. How many times had he heard them sing without music to praise God's name. Hundreds of times. He and Fannie had joined their voices at the singings for the young people, too. Could they do it again?

Noah slapped Walter's shoulder. "The singer has given me an idea. Bishop Lapp said no *Englisch* music, but singing is acceptable to us."

Noah hurried to where Simon Beachy was sitting on the bleachers waiting his turn at bat. "Simon, do you have your cell phone with you? I left mine in the locker room."

Simon glanced up into the stands. "I kind of told my *onkel* I wouldn't use it when he's watching."

"You aren't going to use it, I am."

"It's in the side pocket of my jacket at the end of the bench. Check my messages for me, will you?"

"Sure thing." Noah fished out the phone and

sat on the end of the bench as he dialed Paul's number. "Pick up, cousin. Pick up."

"*Hallo, wee gats*, Simon."

"It's not Simon, it's Noah. I had to use his phone. Are you still in the city?"

"I'm packing up now. We raised a lot of money for Debra's charity and I had a great time."

"*Goot.* Instead of going home, do you think you could take your portable speaker to the horse show?"

"Debra has planned on taking me there, but why bring my speaker?"

"I'll explain later. I've got a game to pitch. Find Timothy when you get there and tell him I'll call him as soon as I'm done."

"Is this about Fannie?"

"*Ja.* This is about her Amish Girls."

"*Mamm* heard from Belinda that Fannie will be there. The doctor has released her to travel."

Relief made Noah's spirits soar. He was going to see her today. He had one more chance to make her see how much he cared. "That is the best news I've had in weeks. *Danki.*"

Noah smiled as he ended the call. He tossed the phone to Simon. "No messages."

Simon slipped the phone under the bench and grabbed his glove. It was their turn to take the field.

Noah jogged out with Walter. "Three up, three

down. That's the plan. I want to end this game as quick as we can."

Walter blew out a deep breath. "You won't get any argument from me. All I ask is that you make me look good. Captain says there are at least six major-league scouts here to check out the country boys."

Noah glanced to where his family was seated in the stands. By their simple life and commitment to God, they stood apart from others. They were in the world, but not a part of it. Living a simple life wasn't simple or easy, but they did it by caring for one another and sharing their burdens and joys.

As he wanted to share Fannie's problems and delights for the rest of their lives.

He had been wrong. He had a lot to go home to. His family and his Amish faith were gifts from God, just as surely as his fastball. He had been waiting for a sign from God to show him where he belonged. The sign had been in front of his eyes all along. He just hadn't seen it because he hadn't been looking for it with his heart. He belonged among the people he loved and cherished. No baseball career was worth giving them up.

A great lightness filled his heart. This was his decision, his God-given gift of free will, and it was the right decision—even if Fannie didn't want to be a part of his life. But he prayed fervently that she would.

The game didn't end as quickly as he would have liked. When it did, the Fire Eaters came out on top and were advanced to the next round. The following morning they would play the winner of the next game.

Back in the locker room, Noah quickly changed into his Amish clothes and pulled out his cell phone to call Connie, who gave her phone to Timothy. After explaining his plan, he hung up and grabbed his ball cap. He stuffed it in his bag and pulled his black Amish hat out.

Eric came in grinning from ear to ear. "Noah, I was just talking to an old friend of mine. He's a scout for the Pittsburgh Pirates these days. He talking to another player now, but he wants to meet you."

Noah drew a deep breath knowing he was about to disappoint his coach. "Walter is the fellow he should talk to."

Eric rested his hands on Noah's shoulders and gave him a shake. "He wants to meet both of you."

"That's great. I'm really glad for Walter, but I have made my decision. I won't be playing after this tournament is over. God has shown me the path He wants me to follow. I'm going home."

Eric's smile faded. "I'm sad to hear that, but I'm happy for you, too. I admire your choice."

Noah settled his broad black hat on his head. "*Danki.* Please excuse me. I've got to get to a horse show."

Fannie walked gingerly into the stands at the exhibition hall. Walking was still painful, and she had to use two canes to keep her balance. Her parents hovered on either side of her.

The music came up and a drill team emerged from the entrance onto the floor of the huge arena. There were ten boys and girls in sparkling cowboy costumes riding quarter horses with decorated saddles.

"Flashy," her father mumbled.

"They are not judged on their costumes, only on how well they ride," she reminded him.

"Are your girls going to be judged?"

"They aren't in the competition. They're going to be featured in the breed spotlight. It is Connie's intention to show how versatile Haflinger horses are."

Fannie's mother waved to someone behind her. "I see Anna and Isaac. They are coming this way."

Fannie closed her eyes. "Is Noah with them?"

"I don't see him, but all the rest of the family

is here. His game must be over. I wonder if our fellows won."

Fannie wondered if God had given Noah the answer he longed for. She prayed he wouldn't be leaving them. She prayed she would have one more chance to mend the rift her pride had caused.

Noah found Timothy with Connie and the girls in the staging area. They were already on their horses. "Did you tell them?" he asked his brother.

"Ja." Timothy nodded.

"It's a wonderful idea. I don't know why we didn't think of it sooner. I could just hug you," Connie said with a wide grin.

Zoe moved her horse closer. She was wearing a dark pink shirt with white fringe along the sleeves and a white kerchief over her hair. Unlike the rest of the girls, her long blond hair hung down her back. "Since we're going to be using 'She'll Be Coming 'Round the Mountain' again, can we add my trick?"

Connie bit her lip. "I don't know, honey. It's so last-minute."

"We've been practicing. We can do it, can't we?" Zoe asked the other riders.

Everyone agreed.

"What trick is this?" Noah asked.

Timothy clapped a hand on Noah's shoulder. "You'll have to see it to believe it."

"All right," Connie said. "Get your other saddle, but hurry. Once around and then into the regular routine. Right?"

"You're awesome, Mom." Zoe wheeled her horse and galloped to the back of the staging area.

Timothy beckoned to Susan, who nudged her horse closer. "I think you should still use the whistle. The horses have gotten used to it."

She nodded. "Okay. Are there a lot of people out there?"

Connie patted her knee. "The only people that matter are on horses beside you. Remember, you are a team. Keep your eyes on each other."

They all nodded.

Paul came up to them carrying his portable loudspeaker. "Where do you want me?"

Noah looked around. "I need to find Fannie first."

"She's with her folks on the west side," Connie said.

"How is she?" Noah asked.

Connie smiled at him. "You should go see for yourself."

Noah rubbed his damp palms on his pants legs. "She may not want to see me. She may not want to do this."

Timothy gave him a shove. "You'll never know if you don't get in there."

He shrugged and started up into the stands. If she saw him, she didn't give any sign until he sat down beside her.

"What's up, *karotte oben*?"

Her gaze flew to his face. Her mouth dropped open and then snapped shut. "You know I hate being called a carrottop."

She didn't look upset. She looked almost happy to see him and his hopes grew.

"Sorry, I forgot. How are you?"

"Getting better. Did you win your game?"

"We did. Six to four. We play again tomorrow."

She looked down at her hands. "Were there professional scouts there?"

"They were."

"And what did they say about your pitching?"

"I didn't stay to find out. I had something more important to do."

She looked at him with a puzzled expression. "What was more important than the thing you've wanted for so long?"

"Helping you. The bishop said the group couldn't perform to recorded music. He didn't say anything about not using live singers. My cousin Paul has a mic and loudspeaker."

He gestured to the group coming in. Lillian, Mary, Emma and Rebecca came down to sit behind her with his brothers behind them. Paul sat down beside Fannie.

Fannie looked around at everyone. "I don't understand."

Noah took her hand in his. "We're going to sing with you, Fannie, but first I have to check and see if Connie is ready."

He rose to his feet, but she caught his hand. "Noah, why are you doing this?"

She was so dear to his heart. Didn't she realize that? "Because this is important to you."

"No, why are you doing this?"

He tilted his head to the side. "Don't you know, *liebchen*?"

Fannie's heart was pounding in her chest. "Maybe I do, but tell me anyway."

His grip on her hand tightened as he dropped to one knee beside her. "I'm doing this because what is important to you is important to me. I love you, Fannie. Even if you can't love me back, I still love you and I will never stop loving you."

Joy flooded her heart until she could barely breathe. With all her faults and shortcomings, he still loved her. The knowledge was humbling. "I don't deserve your love."

"I'm sorry. I can't change the way I feel. We'll talk about this later when we don't have such a large audience." He winked and hurried away.

Lillian put her arm around Fannie's shoulders. "Our Lord has filled Noah's heart with love for you, Fannie. You may not feel you deserve it, but *Gott* does not make mistakes. When Noah gets around to proposing, you'd better accept. We want you for our sister."

Tears filled Fannie's eyes as she looked at the women around her. "I'll give it serious consideration."

It would take her all of two seconds to say yes to him if he did propose. She loved him with all her heart and she would spend a lifetime trying to be worthy of God's great gift to her.

A few minutes later, Noah returned. "We're going to do 'She'll Be Coming 'Round the Mountain.' I will start, but at a slower cadence than the recorded song we were using. I want everyone to join in on the second stanza. The girls will come in on the second verse, so we'll speed up then and everyone will sing. I'll keep the time like this." He extended one finger and tapped the air.

Everyone nodded that they understood. "One more thing. Instead of 'driving six white horses,' we'll change it to 'driving six *wild* horses.' Okay?"

"Why?" Fannie asked.

"You'll see."

He raised a hand to signal the announcer in the booth above them and took the microphone from Paul.

The man's voice boomed over the arena's PA system. "Ladies and gentlemen, in our breed showcase this afternoon I'd like to welcome the Stroud Stables Haflingers and their riders, The Amish Girls. They are here to showcase the versatility of this breed. The Haflinger is also known as the Avelignese. The breed was developed in the mountainous regions of Austria and northern Italy during the nineteenth century. Some were brought to the US in the 1950s and the breed has been gaining in popularity since that time.

"Haflingers are relatively small and are considered a pony at 14.2 hands, which is 58 inches or less in height at the withers. These well-muscled ponies are remarkably strong. In fact, the winner of the pony pull yesterday was a pair of Haflingers from Holms County, Ohio. They pulled seventy-two hundred pounds a distance of ten feet ten inches to win the heavyweight division.

"They are always golden in color with white or flaxen manes and tails. The breed has its own distinctive gait described by enthusiasts as energetic but smooth. If you haven't heard of Haflingers before, after today I'm sure you'll agree this is no ordinary horse and these are no ordinary riders. I'm pleased to present the Stroud Stables Haflingers and The Amish Girls."

"She'll be coming 'round the mountain when

she comes." Noah's pure baritone voice poured out of the speaker. He nodded to Fannie.

She leaned in to add her voice to his. "She'll be coming 'round the mountain when she comes."

As they sang together, Fannie's heart grew light. She loved him so much. She couldn't wait to say those words to him.

She turned her attention to the arena entrance at the end of the stanza. The sharp crack of a whip shattered the quiet, and Noah motioned for his brothers and their wives to pick up the tempo and sing.

"She'll be driving six wild horses when she comes." Their blend of voices filled the air as horses and riders charged into the arena. They came six abreast with two singles in line behind them. Fannie saw Zoe on the first single horse. She was riding Misty. Abbie followed close behind her on Copper.

Zoe shot to her feet in a hippodrome stand. She was grinning from ear to ear and held a buggy whip in her right hand. She cracked it once as if driving the six horses in front of her and then waved to the stands as she raced past. The crowd erupted into cheers. Fannie could hardly believe her eyes. Zoe was a born performer.

After a thundering run around the perimeter, the girls slowed and broke into two columns as they began the routine Fannie had worked so hard to perfect. They did it beautifully, and in time with the singing, as Susan marked each change of pattern with a burst from her whistle.

It was a sight to behold—eight matching golden-caramel-colored horses with bright blond manes and tails stepping lightly in response to the Amish girls on their backs.

Fannie held her breath when they began their pass through the jumps, but every hurdle was cleared easily. When the last turn was made and the riders were leaving the arena, the crowd rose to its feet with deafening applause.

The announcer came back on when the noise died away. "Ladies and gentlemen, as impressive as that was, it's not all these girls and their horses can do. In a minute, we'll have a demonstration of their skill in harness. These will be the same horses and drivers with one exception. We will have one change of driver because the mother of the little gal who rides standing up tells us she isn't old enough to drive." The audience laughed.

Zoe came out leading Misty, who had been harnessed to a two-wheeled cart. She stopped in front of Noah and Fannie.

Noah leaned down to whisper in Fannie's ear. "Are you ready?"

"For what?"

"You started this wonderful crazy adventure.

You must have a hand in the finish." He gently slipped his arms beneath her and picked her up.

Tears stung her eyes. "You want me to ride with you?"

"I want you to drive. After all, you can drive almost as well as I can."

She pulled back, a smile trembling on her lips. "Almost?"

"How about *just* as well?"

"*Ja*, Noah Bowman, that is more like it. I think you are beginning to understand me."

"Now that is a scary thought."

His brother Samuel opened the gate leading to the arena floor. Noah carried Fannie through and placed her tenderly on the seat of the cart. Zoe handed her the reins. Misty tossed her head, eager to be off again.

Noah covered Fannie's hand. "Are you sure you are well enough to do this?"

She gazed into his eyes. "As long as I have someone by my side to steady me, I will be fine."

He smiled. "Can I volunteer for the job?"

"I was hoping you would." Her heart was beating so hard that she was amazed he couldn't heart it.

"I want to spend a lifetime by your side, Fannie. You believe that, don't you?"

"I do. I love you will all my heart and soul, Noah Bowman."

His closed his eyes for a long second, as though savoring her words. Finally, he gazed at her tenderly. "Will you marry me?"

"Gladly. Oh, so gladly. *Gott* has chosen us for one another."

"If we weren't in front of so many people I would kiss you, Fannie Erb."

"Well, stop dawdling and get in so we can finish the program and find someplace more private."

He laughed as he went around and climbed in beside her. "That, my love, is your best idea to date."

Noah pulled his buggy to a stop in front of Fannie's house one month after her accident. Before he could get down, she was already out the door. She still moved stiffly in her back brace, but she wasn't letting it slow her any.

"You're late," she called out.

"You're rude," he snapped back, trying to stifle a grin.

"Just making sure you don't think I've mellowed."

"No chance of that, *karotte oben*."

She climbed in gingerly beside him. "You know I hate that name."

"That's why I use it."

She smiled and lifted her face for his kiss. He

eagerly complied as she slipped her arms around his neck.

Kissing Fannie would never get old. The wedding couldn't come soon enough. They would finish their baptismal classes in another month and take their vows of faith soon after. The wedding would be the second Thursday in November. Not nearly soon enough.

Finally, he drew back. "You are making us even later."

"You've got a fast horse. You can make up the time." She pulled him down for another quick kiss, then straightened in her seat and made shooing motions with her hands. "What are you waiting for? Get a move on."

"You drive me crazy, woman."

"And you love it." She winked at him.

He flicked the reins. "What did I do to deserve this?"

She linked her arm through his. "You came to my rescue like a knight of old."

"Timothy would say that's proof you weren't paying attention in history class. There weren't any Amish knights."

Laying her head on his shoulder, she sighed. "But there were many brave Amish heroes, and I have one of my very own."

He headed Willy toward Connie's farm. "We

aren't married yet. I could change my mind and court Margret Stolfus."

"You won't."

"What makes you so sure?"

"She married Hiram yesterday. Didn't you hear?"

"Are you kidding me?"

"Nope."

"That was one rushed wedding."

"I'm sure Hiram didn't want another fiancée to change her mind."

"How is your sister?"

"Happy as a clam at the seashore. All she can talk about in her letters is the wonderful Mennonite fellow she met at the beach. She wrote that she tried to stop seeing him as our parents asked, but her heart overruled her head. I expect they will marry soon."

"How do your parents feel about that?"

"She hasn't been baptized. They aren't thrilled that she won't be Amish, but an Old Order Mennonite is close enough. Apparently, the Amish community down there is more open. My grandparents both like him, so that helps. Betsy wants us to come visit them on our wedding trip."

"I had planned to take you to see your grandparents, but we are not taking Trinket with us and that is final."

"As you wish."

"Come again? Are you sick?"

"I'm simply agreeing with you."

"That's what worries me." He eyed her with concern.

"Have you heard from Walter?"

"Another happy clam. He's been signed to a minor-league team, but I know he'll be called up to the majors before too long."

"At least a few good things came out of our deception."

"Our one and only deception. From now on, we are walking a straight path together."

"I couldn't agree more."

He turned into Connie's lane. A horse trailer and pickup were sitting next to the barn. Zoe was waiting beside the truck cab. She dashed toward them. "I thought you would never get here."

Connie came around from the back of the trailer. "Calm down, Zoe. We have plenty of time. Help Noah stable his horse and then get your gear."

Zoe rolled her eyes. "It's been in the truck since I got up this morning, Mom."

As she and Noah led Willy away, Connie gave Fannie a gentle hug. "How are you?"

"Getting better every day. How are you?"

"Better than I've been in a long time. I sold three horses this week and two the week before. The two last week went to a therapy program run by a very nice, very cute single man who has asked me out. Oh, and I finally fired George. I hired a new guy full-time to run things while Zoe and I are on the road."

"Oh, Connie, I'm so happy for you."

"Aren't you going to ask me who the new guy is?"

"Do I know him?"

"Quite well," Noah said, grinning like the cat that ate the canary.

"You?" Fannie stared at him in stunned shock. "What about your family's business? The farm?"

"With my cousins moving here permanently, there is plenty of help in the woodshop and on the farm. Besides, I'll only be two miles away if they need me. I've found I have a passion for Haflinger horses and a crazy woman who can tame a horse by turning in circles. As my wife, you will have to help me with my work. I expect there will be many times when we must ride together to exercise the horses. Perhaps we can even convince the bishop that horseback riding isn't worldly but a *goot* plain way to enjoy a family outing. You might want to think about where we should build our house."

Fannie leaned forward and kissed him. "I will."

Connie cleared her throat. "Our participation in the show impressed a number of people. Zoe tells me the video went viral, which I assume is good although it sounds horrible. I've been getting calls all week. Six more families have enrolled their kids in my riding classes, so you will be busy when you get out of that brace. I have you to thank for lifting some of the weight from my shoulders."

"I'm happy it turned out well for you."

"It didn't turn out too badly for you, either. He's a good man. You two will do well in harness together."

Zoe came running out of the barn. She opened the cab of the truck. "Let's go. I can't be late for my first paying gig. I'm so glad you are coming to watch me, Fannie. And you, too, Noah. I'm going to be awesome."

She leaned over to whisper to Fannie. "I'm trying to convince Mom to make us a mother-daughter act, but she's dragging her feet."

Connie shook her head. "I have created a monster. She's determined to become the best trick rider in the world and the halftime show at the Carlson rodeo will be her jumping-off point, if we get her there on time."

Noah opened the back door of the cab. "A very large goal for a small girl."

"One that I'm sure she will accomplish with *Gott*'s help," Fannie said.

Connie's smile faded. "I can't begin to thank the two of you for all you have done for us." She walked quickly to the driver's side of the truck and got in.

"Who would have thought our pretend courtship could open so many doors?" Fannie said softly.

Noah laid his hand on Fannie's cheek. "Do you know the most amazing thing about it?"

She shook her head.

He stroked her lips with his thumb. "It wasn't a pretend courtship at all. The Lord does move in mysterious ways."

"I love you, Noah Bowman."

"I love you, *karotte oben*."

"And I hope all your kids are redheads," Zoe said with a giggle before her mother shushed her.

* * * * *

If you enjoyed
THEIR PRETEND AMISH COURTSHIP,
look for the other books in the
AMISH BACHELORS *series:*

AN AMISH HARVEST
AN AMISH NOEL
HIS AMISH TEACHER

Dear Reader,

Fannie and Noah have become my most favorite characters to date. And after thirty books, that's a lot of characters. This young couple are not the most mature people, but they both have good hearts. Their dedication to their friends is what drew me to them the most.

Fannie's temper is something I can identify with, for I raised a hothead, too, although she wasn't a redhead. My poor daughter had many mouth-before-brain moments. Fortunately, she grew out of that temper and is now as easygoing as I am. Almost.

Fannie and Noah were at the opposite ends of their faith journey. Noah believed wholeheartedly that God would show him the path to take. In his unwavering belief, he forgot that the Lord gave us free will. We have a say in our fates. We make the choices that change our lives.

Fannie was at the other extreme. She believed, but her faith was shallow. She thought she could make life happen as she wanted because she wanted it. She forgot that nothing is possible without God's help. Nothing. Knowing God and not asking for His help is like owning a cell phone and not using it to call 911 when you're in a car wreck. Prayer is a tool. Use it.

I hope you enjoyed their story and I want to let you know my next book, *Amish Christmas Twins*, will be out in time for... You guessed it... Christmas.

Blessings to you and yours,

Patricia Davids

Get 2 Free Books,
Plus 2 Free Gifts—
just for trying the Reader Service!

Get 2 Free Books,
Plus 2 Free Gifts—
just for trying the
Reader Service!

YES! Please send me 2 FREE Harlequin® Heartwarming™ Larger-Print novels and my 2 FREE mystery gifts (gifts worth about $10 retail). After receiving them, if I don't wish to receive any more books, I can return the shipping statement marked "cancel." If I don't cancel, I will receive 4 brand-new larger-print novels every month and be billed just $5.49 per book in the U.S. or $6.24 per book in Canada. That's a savings of at least 19% off the cover price. It's quite a bargain! Shipping and handling is just 50¢ per book in the U.S. and 75¢ per book in Canada.* I understand that accepting the 2 free books and gifts places me under no obligation to buy anything. I can always return a shipment and cancel at any time. Even if I never buy another book, the 2 free books and gifts are mine to keep forever.

161/361 IDN GLQL

Name	(PLEASE PRINT)

Address	Apt. #

City	State/Prov.	Zip/Postal Code

Signature (if under 18, a parent or guardian must sign)

Mail to the **Reader Service:**
IN U.S.A.: P.O. Box 1867, Buffalo, NY 14240-1867
IN CANADA: P.O. Box 611, Fort Erie, Ontario L2A 9Z9

Want to try two free books from another line?
Call 1-800-873-8635 today or visit www.ReaderService.com.

* Terms and prices subject to change without notice. Prices do not include applicable taxes. Sales tax applicable in N.Y. Canadian residents will be charged applicable taxes. Offer not valid in Quebec. This offer is limited to one order per household. Books received may not be as shown. Not valid for current subscribers to Harlequin Heartwarming Larger-Print books. All orders subject to credit approval. Credit or debit balances in a customer's account(s) may be offset by any other outstanding balance owed by or to the customer. Please allow 4 to 6 weeks for delivery. Offer available while quantities last.

Your Privacy—The Reader Service is committed to protecting your privacy. Our Privacy Policy is available online at www.ReaderService.com or upon request from the Reader Service.

We make a portion of our mailing list available to reputable third parties that offer products we believe may interest you. If you prefer that we not exchange your name with third parties, or if you wish to clarify or modify your communication preferences, please visit us at www.ReaderService.com/consumerchoice or write to us at Reader Service Preference Service, P.O. Box 9062, Buffalo, NY 14240-9062. Include your complete name and address.

HOMETOWN HEARTS ♥

YES! Please send me **The Hometown Hearts Collection** in Larger Print. This collection begins with 3 FREE books and 2 FREE gifts in the first shipment. Along with my 3 free books, I'll also get the next 4 books from the Hometown Hearts Collection, in LARGER PRINT, which I may either return and owe nothing, or keep for the low price of $4.99 U.S./ $5.89 CDN each plus $2.99 for shipping and handling per shipment*. If I decide to continue, about once a month for 8 months I will get 6 or 7 more books, but will only need to pay for 4. That means 2 or 3 books in every shipment will be FREE! If I decide to keep the entire collection, I'll have paid for only 32 books because 19 books are FREE! I understand that accepting the 3 free books and gifts places me under no obligation to buy anything. I can always return a shipment and cancel at any time. My free books and gifts are mine to keep no matter what I decide.

262 HCN 3432 462 HCN 3432

Name	(PLEASE PRINT)	
Address		Apt. #
City	State/Prov.	Zip/Postal Code

Signature (if under 18, a parent or guardian must sign)

Mail to the **Reader Service**:

IN U.S.A.: P.O. Box 1867, Buffalo, NY. 14240-1867
IN CANADA: P.O. Box 609, Fort Erie, Ontario L2A 5X3

READERSERVICE.COM

Manage your account online!

- Review your order history
- Manage your payments
- Update your address

> **We've designed the
> Reader Service website
> just for you.**

Enjoy all the features!

- Discover new series available to you, and read excerpts from any series.
- Respond to mailings and special monthly offers.
- Browse the Bonus Bucks catalog and online-only exculsives.
- Share your feedback.

Visit us at:

ReaderService.com

RS16R